'JUST A REMINDER- EACH DAY'

Book 1 - January to June

TANYA C WHITTAKER

NATIONAL
LIBRARY
OF AUSTRALIA

A catalogue record for this book is available from the National Library of Australia

Publisher:
Inspiring Publishers
P.O. Box 159, Calwell, ACT Australia 2905
Email: inspiringpublisher.com
http://www.inspiringpublishers.com

National Library of Australia Cataloguing-in-Publication entry

Author: Tanya C Whittaker

Title: **'JUST A REMINDER-EACH DAY'**
    Book 1 – January to June

ISBN: 978-1-922920-19-5 (Print)

PREFACE

A mystery that affects most people is the existence of God. Many people believe there is a higher authority but, in believing, we still want proof - a sense that this spiritual identity is a relational God, one who not only listens to us personally but also speaks to us. I admit that I 'hang out' to hear God speak to me, to have confirmation that he knows me and has a good purpose for my life. Along the journey of writing these daily devotions, I have had my ups and downs. Some days it seemed clear that God was giving me something specific to write and other days I wondered! Although most entries started out as stories their purpose was always to draw the reader's attention to a Bible verse. Amazingly, with my Bible laid open, sometimes all day, trying to find the right reading for a particular story, I have experienced fulfilment in a totally new way. Overall, it has turned out to be quite different from organising Christian events, horse riding and the farm activities that usually occupy my life.

Some statistics, randomly chosen, regarding the number of people who read their Bible, indicate that 11% of Americans, 9% of British and 8% of Australians are fairly regular Bible readers.

A 2002 survey found that 29% of Australian adults still read the Bible at least once a year, and interestingly, in 2010, around 10% of Australian secondary students admitted to reading the Bible weekly or more, and a further 15 to 20% browsed it occasionally. Some surveys reveal that people who read their Bible every day are less inclined towards destructive life choices. On a more positive note, daily Bible reading can offer wisdom, guidance, hope, healing, comfort, insight into truth, discernment, deliverance, and help in resisting temptation.

Considering our modern-day distractions are numerous, it is quite possible we don't know how to get started or even know how to enjoy daily Bible reading. We may need some encouragement with a story we can relate to that draws us to the Bible. With 1,839 Bible versions available in 1,275 languages we would surely find one that meets our specific needs.

While I am convinced that God's living word is highly valuable for us daily, I hope this book is more than just some of my personal experiences with God and it becomes God's opportunity to reveal more of himself to the reader.

'Just a Reminder-Each Day'

ABOUT THE AUTHOR

Tanya grew up in country South Australia, enjoying horse riding in its many forms but unaware of her need for God. Life for Tanya included Pony Club, Show Riding, Dressage, Hunting and Polocrosse.

With the support of her inspiring mother, this led her to some exciting adventures. After marrying Phil, she became a Christian. This life-changing experience took her out of her comfort zone. She struggled to adapt to going to church instead of riding horses on Sundays, but at the same time, she was eager to learn more about life with Jesus. In her search, she could not find a daily Bible reading book to which she could relate. The Holy Spirit has faithfully led Tanya on a journey of discovery.

Tanya and Phil have farmed together, organised youth camps and led church services most of their married life. After a friend prayed for Tanya, she felt a strong urge to write a book of 365 daily devotions with the understanding that God would provide the ideas.

The coming together of these Bible reflections and true stories, 'Just a Reminder-Each Day, January to June,' offers the reader insight, guidance and some special moments with God.

Scriptures are taken from the NIV New International Version of the Holy Bible, 1978 by Biblica.

ACKNOWLEDGMENTS

In this new venture as a writer, I have received encouragement and many positive words at the right time. I am very thankful to the following people. Successful author, Roger Norris-Green, for his genuine guidance whenever I have needed it. To Debbie and Jan for their assistance in editing and my husband Phil and our extended family and friends for their patience, prayerful support and encouragement. I am very grateful to my mother, Naomi, who enabled me to have many horse-riding adventures. I thank God that he has given me an enjoyable challenge when I least expected something new in my life. Thank you also to Peter K for his inspirational prayer which initiated this project and to the people who have shaped my faith, enabling me to write *Just a Reminder-Each Day, January to June.* *Tanya*

Photo used for March 22, with much appreciation,
by photographer Liz Davis.

'Just a Reminder-Each Day'

New Day - New Beginning

New Year's Day usually presents an opportunity for a new beginning.

Even Mondays can feel like a new beginning and setting out on a holiday is even better. We are a species that needs to turn a page, do something different, try something new or leave something behind.

The dawn of a new day may be all we need to experience renewed hope. After Jesus had ascended, his bewildered, confused and saddened followers waited with little understanding of what lay ahead. When his Spirit did appear, it was one of the most amazing events the followers of Jesus had encountered. It was a big crowd event for everyone to see but also unique; it was personal as each person felt the wind of the Holy Spirit come on them, enabling them to speak in tongues. They were elevated to another level in their faith, like hope turning into a sure thing. (*Acts 2: 1-4*)

Jesus was now with them in the form of his Spirit, a daily experience that would stay with them forever. It was a new day with an entirely unexpected new experience. When we need to turn a new page, leave yesterday behind and find something new, the renewing of His Spirit in us enables us to experience the unexpected.

"Lord God, by the power of your Holy Spirit, please refresh us today and give us renewed hope. Please pour out your Spirit on our community and nation to renew our hope in you. Thank you, Jesus."

Lamentations 3: 22,23
Because of the Lord's great love we are not consumed, for his compassions never fail. They are new every morning; great is your faithfulness.

January 2
Forgiveness

We don't think about forgiveness until there is something to forgive. Some things are easy to forgive, while others can be incredibly hard. It is sad to hear people say, "I will never forgive." Forgiving can be associated with excusing the wrong or saying it doesn't matter.

Understandably, some people refuse to forgive, but it can cause lasting damage. A wrong is a wrong, whether it is forgiven or not. What matters is the mental and spiritual health of the people involved. To be forgiven allows us to move on. To forgive not only sets the offender free but also sets the victim free from harbouring unforgiveness, which is a heavy burden to carry.

God's example of forgiveness is our benchmark in that Jesus, his son, died for every type of bad behaviour. He set the rule in place - forgive as your heavenly father forgave you. Unforgiveness may lie hidden, but it still hurts; it can cripple us, wreck relationships, and limit our ability to move into new relationships with an open heart. Unforgiveness can be a wedge between God and us because, unconsciously we know God asks us to forgive and get on with life.

A lady once borrowed a little dress from me for her daughter. It was one that my daughter had outgrown, but years later, when the dress would not be of any value to her, I asked for it back. She told me I did not need it. The dress was given to my daughter by my grandmother, so it had a deeper meaning to me. I struggled to forgive this lady but eventually, I left it in God's hands. One day, unexpectedly, the lady returned the dress. There were a lot of emotions tied up in that simple little event, and the return of the dress was a sweet closure.

"Lord God, please help us to forgive for our sakes. Thank you for your constant forgiveness, which releases us daily to live in freedom. Thank you, Jesus."

Colossians 3:13
Bear with each other and forgive whatever grievances you may have against one another.

Matthew 18:21
Then Peter came to Jesus and asked, "Lord how many times shall I forgive my brother when he sins against me? Up to seven times?" Jesus answered, "I tell you, not seven times but seventy-seven times."

'Just a Reminder-Each Day'

In the Silence

When city and suburban people pack their cars and load up their families to escape their noisy, busy lives, the country is where they go. There is nothing like silence! Perfect silence is not really what we aim for. It is the gentle rustle of treetops, the almost silent lap of small waves arriving on the shore and the fluttering noise of birds moving from tree to tree that we call silence, believable silence.

Some people believe that God speaks in a gentle whisper (1 Kings 19: 12). Others want to hear from God in a loud, invigorating voice (Revelation 1: 15). In the silence, God makes himself heard, especially for those desiring to hear. In the noise of life, God still makes himself heard by those wishing to hear. Silence is a huge blessing when we need that uncluttered space, but it is not for everyone. The good news is that God meets us where it suits us, too.

"Lord God, the silence of your creation, when undisturbed by too many of us human beings, is a national treasure for those who can spend some time in the country. We thank you so much for each moment we have spent in the silence of your creation. Thank you, Jesus."

John 10: 27,28
My sheep listen to my voice; I know them, and they follow me. I give them eternal life, and they shall never perish; no-one can snatch them out of my hand.

'Just a Reminder-Each Day'

Relationships

Relationships can be hard. Some people thrive on friendships, some can't live without people around them all the time, some like to be alone, while others enjoy company occasionally. All of us need someone sometimes. The problem with friendships is our differences. We can rub each other the wrong way or complement each other.

The good times in relationships are occasions that we talk about for ages afterwards. The secret to having good and lasting friendships must be in our ability to overlook our differences, be forgiving, be generous in contributing to each other's lives and be grateful for our friends. If we see each other as one of God's people, regardless of whether they acknowledge God or not, we are more likely to like them, if not love them.

Men and women weren't meant to be totally alone. Friendships are a vital part of life. Having a friendship with God's Spirit brings another dimension into friendships. He enriches our human relationships. The Holy Spirit is a mediator; he goes between us, directing our thoughts and helping us to see and know people on a deeper level. Being open to the Holy Spirit enables him to give quality to our human friendships and enhance our walk with God.

"Lord God, please teach us to appreciate the people around us. Please give us wisdom in what we say and the ability to forgive rather than be

offended. Please help others to bear with us when we slip up. Thank you for the people who form our network of friends, and please keep our relationships healthy. Thank you, Jesus."

Ephesians 4: 2
Be completely humble and gentle; be patient, bearing with one another in love. Make every effort to keep the unity of the Spirit through the bond of peace.

January 5

Victim to Victory

'**S**elf-pity is a sin'. I don't know if I read this or heard it preached but it made me cross. I had a right to feel sorry for myself! I was the victim, and I still carried the scars. Even though verbal abuse was a thing of my past, I still shuddered when people raised their voices. After years of living in an unhappy situation, my mother made a wise decision to move us out. We went to live in a place where life changed from fear to fun.

Much later, after being happily married for years, I knew deep down that I still felt sorry for myself. I struggled to cope as well as other young mums. I used self-pity as a means of comforting myself. The problem was, could I go on feeling sorry for myself when I knew I was growing in spiritual strength? Thanks to God and support from family and friends, I was getting stronger.

At some stage, I came to a fork in the road. I chose to walk down the path of victory and leave the path of the victim behind. Slowly, I was being healed. I knew it was by God's design, wanting the best for me, that I had made progress. I don't believe God accuses us of self-pity to get us out of the bog! (Farm term, referring to vehicles getting stuck in the mud!).

I feel sure Jesus wanted us to see God's strength and compassion, especially for victims when he referred to God as Father, the great Dad who builds his children up and gives them security.

"Lord God, please help me recognise that you make me stronger. Thank you for healing any broken parts in my life. Thank you for giving me the desire to be victorious rather than remain the victim who wants to be pitied. Thank you, Jesus."

1 Corinthians 15: 57
But thanks be to God! He gives us the victory through our Lord Jesus Christ.

✦

January 6
Unforeseen

The woman on the other end of the telephone was apologetically telling me there were no more cabins available in her caravan park. As she was talking, I sensed some sympathy when she said adding that the cabin for disabled guests had not been booked. "We can put you there if you don't mind," she said. I could not see why it wouldn't work, so I happily accepted her offer.

It was fun when our grandchildren turned up at our cabin door. Their caravan was positioned at a friend's house three blocks from the fore-shore where we were staying. One morning, the youngest grandson knocked at the door with an urgent appeal. His older brother had fallen off his bike and was crying. We ran to his aid and saw the skid marks down the steep gravel track that led into the park. Our other grandson was sitting holding his bleeding knees; his abandoned bike lay on its side where it fell. With a comforting arm, we helped him back to our cabin, which just happened to be very close to the entrance. All the while, I wondered how I would fix the damaged, bleeding knees with bits of gravel still stuck to them. the youngest grandson brought the bike back and leaned it against the decking. Grandpa was sent on a mission to find the first aid kit from under the car seat while I seated the patient in the huge bathroom for disabled people. It was beginning to dawn on me why we were meant to have this cabin. I reached for the extendable shower head and gently washed the blood and gravel off. It wasn't long before the patient was dried, bandaged and happily having morning tea with us. During this time, his younger brother was continuously recapping the event, how the bike just slid out of control and how his brother just slid in the opposite direction! I was secretly praising God, who made it so easy for us to care for our injured grandson.

"Lord God, it is hard to understand everything that happens in our lives. Some things frustrate us because we can't see the bigger picture, but please help us to be able to trust you even when we can't see ahead. Thank you, Jesus."

John 13: 5-7 (In this Bible reading, Peter is unsure why Jesus wants to stoop down and wash his feet.)
After that, he poured water in a basin and began to wash his disciples' feet, drying them with the towel he had wrapped around him. He came to Simon Peter, who said to him, "Lord are you going to wash my feet?" Jesus replied, "You do not realise now what I am doing, but later you will understand."

Thanks, Mate!

After getting ourselves into an awkward position, trying to find a park for our 4WD and long caravan in a small car park, a man on foot called out, "Where do you want to go?" My husband leaned out his window and called back, "Anywhere around here, we just want to go to the shops!" In a casual, helpful style, the man, clearly a local working guy, directed us to a more suitable place to park if we didn't mind walking a short distance. "Thanks, mate," my grateful husband replied, and then he lightly added a comment about the joys of caravanning. We took the man's advice and drove from the awkward car park to the large, shaded area suggested. We agreed it was a nice experience, on top of a rather embarrassing mistake we had made.

The man's casual and happy-to-help attitude did us a heap of good. Thanks to God. I wondered if the man knew what a blessing he was to us. We agreed that a good response would be to pray for him and his family. Later that evening, we prayed that God would take care of them with healing, fulfilment, happiness and salvation. We often think those awkward situations are sent to try us, but maybe they are sent so that we may bless someone.

"Lord God, thank you for all the people who have helped us out of awkward situations: our parents, friends, and family, as well as strangers. Thank you, Jesus."

Proverbs 12: 25
An anxious heart weighs a man down, but a kind word cheers him up.

'Just a Reminder-Each Day'

He Works in Me

To this end, I labour, struggling with all his energy, which so powerfully works in me. (Colossians 1:29)

I often wonder why Paul uses the term, 'the mystery of the gospel' – but this verse is impressive when we consider the energy of God working in a human being to do what God wants to be done.

The moth struggles to come out of its cocoon, chickens struggle to get out of the egg, (an analogy of the born-again experience); giving birth can be a massive struggle for many species, including humans. Paul admits it is a struggle to keep powering on to get people set for heaven, to convince them to trust in Jesus, yet he admits God's energy empowers him. Some Christians are driven to convert people. Still, the same energy from God is at work in others to conserve the planet, discover medical cures, fight wars and bring justice and harmony where there is discourse. That same power is at work in us when we teach children, care for the aged, grow gardens, rescue animals and foster lost and lonely souls.

It is a huge mystery how the power of God can work in any of us, but the disciples understood this when the Holy Spirit came upon them at Pentecost. They experienced something out of the ordinary, just as Jesus promised. The amazing thing about God's empowerment is its lasting effect on people throughout their lives and its availability for each generation. It is the same Spirit at work in all of us for our good and God's purposes.

"Lord God, what a mystery it is that you choose to empower us with your Holy Spirit. But at the same time, we want to be on this exciting journey with you. Please help us to use your power to do the good you would have us do. Thank you, Jesus."

Acts 19: 6
When Paul placed his hands on them, the Holy Spirit came on them, and they spoke in tongues and prophesied.

'Just a Reminder-Each Day'

January 9
Sloppy Joe's

Some names, terms, songs, statements and conversations take us directly back to their origin. When I hear the word 'Sloppy Joe', I am immediately transported back to the 1960s. Owning a Sloppy Joe jumper was really cool! We wore our Sloppy Joes with pride. The longer and sloppier they were (within reason), the better they were, especially when worn with shorts. And in those days they were short shorts! So, by now you've got it - the Sloppy Joe covered the shorts and it appeared the teenager was only wearing a jumper! Long sleeves, a long body and bulky knit describe a Sloppy Joe from the 1960s. My teen years were very happy and the thought of wearing a Sloppy Joe makes me happy.

It is beneficial to think about our good 'God' experiences and think about them often. If we can reflect on a time and place where we have had a positive experience of God's love and encouragement, it does us good. It may have been a significant revelation, some good teaching that spurred us on or a fun time with friends that built our faith. Remember the goodness of God, the welcoming love of the Father, the gutsy sacrifice Jesus made for us and the friendship we have with his Holy Spirit.

"Lord God, please forgive us when we forget about your goodness and all the encouraging things you have done for us. Please remind us that

you are there and can bring us back whenever we wander or lose sight of you. Thank you, Jesus."

Palm 77: 11,12
I will remember the deeds of the Lord; yes, I will remember your miracles of long ago. I will meditate on all your works and consider all your mighty deeds.

Bless this House

My mother was able to buy a classic old limestone house that had a fascinating history. It was a haven for my mother and me after her relationship with my stepfather broke down. The home was badly in need of repairs. It had been treated poorly by the previous tenants. My mother accepted the challenge, and over the years, she brought the house back to its former glory. Mum always had a project on the go, whether it was another oil painting, adding interesting detail to the interior of the home or developing the garden way beyond the house. People visited her art gallery and admired the historic 'Gum Flat Homestead'.

After I married, my husband and I visited my mother regularly and enjoyed the nicely renovated and personalised home that was once in bad shape. On one visit, we had our married daughter and two grandchildren with us. We had shared a meal, and the grandchildren had enjoyed playing with the toys Mum had set out.

Positioned just inside the front door, Mum had a statue of a regal-looking lion. She also had her saddle, perched on a saddle rack, giving character to the long passageway. The lion was used as a hatstand for her riding hat. It looked quite impressive, but just as we said goodbye and walked out the wide carpeted passageway, our granddaughter turned back and straightened the riding hat on the lion's head. We watched the 3-year-old with fascination, trying to understand her actions, and concluded that she wanted to leave the hat looking as good as when we first arrived.

"Lord God, being hospitable is your desire for all of us. Please help us to have homes that bless others. Thank you, Jesus."

Matthew 10: 11,12,13
Whatever town or village you enter, search for some worthy person there and stay at his house until you leave. As you enter the home, give it your greeting. If the home is deserving, let your peace rest on it; if it is not, let your peace return to you.

'Just a Reminder-Each Day'

January 11
Love Affirms

With an engagement card open, ready to write on, my thoughts went at once to 'Congratulations'; That part was easy, but then I got sidetracked, remembering the first time I saw the couple together. They are people we have known for a long time.

We have had the enjoyment of seeing their affection for each other grow. It is a familiar human experience where two people develop confidence in each other. They spend more and more time together and often change from hanging out with the crowd to preferring to be alone with each other. In good relationships, the couple navigates their way into each other's lives, spending a lot of time talking. They cover many subjects, gradually realising that they either agree on their likes and dislikes or at least appreciate their differences enough to want more of each other's company. Couples in love are nice people to be with. There is usually a certain amount of affirmation between them. They want the best for each other, are keen to keep their relationship going and tend to see each other through rose-coloured glasses.

The relationship God wants for us is also one of affirming love. He wants his people to know they can trust him, that he has their best interests at heart, and that he wants the relationship to flourish and last. His love is pure and faultless and always directed towards us. He does not see us through rose-coloured glasses but with unconditional

27

love that deliberately overlooks our faults. Our part is to enjoy his love and allow it to affect our lives.

"Lord God, We thank you for your unfailing love towards us. Help us to be aware of your faithfulness and to accept your love without fear of being let down. Thank you, Jesus."

1 John 4: 10
This is love; not that we loved God, but that he loved us and sent his Son as an atoning sacrifice for our sins.

January 12

Summertime

Hot days and hot nights! There is so much written about WW11 and the bombing of Darwin. We enjoyed discovering more of this history during our holiday in the Northern Territory.

Each day and night that we were in the city and caravan park outside the city, it was hot, but the tourist spots like the museum and the tunnels were nicely air-conditioned. Enduring the heat revealed what it must have been like for the early settlers and soldiers in that region. Those who worked outside in extremely hot conditions with limited drinking water, mainly using hand tools and no air conditioning to retreat to, must have known tough times.

We were so appreciative of our water bottles and having easy access to shops for more cold drinks and shaded seating. The more we learned about the early days and hardships of living in Darwin, the more we marvelled at the resilience of those people.

There is nothing like extreme situations, tropical humidity, dry heat, deserts and droughts to make us focus on the life-giving ability of water. When Jesus got into conversation with a Samaritan woman at a well (John 4: 7-15), he offered her 'Living water,' water that would go on quenching her thirst right into eternity. He was referring to his Spirit living in her. In a hot, dry place, we long to drink. Water is life-giving and life-saving; we can't live without it. No one can save us like Jesus and be with us through every dry and desperate time in life as our Lord can.

"Lord God, we know the relief of being able to drink when we most need it. Please help us understand how to tap into your living water to trust you with our present needs and future. Thank you, Jesus."

Revelation 22: 1
Then the angel showed me the river of the water of life, as clear as crystal, flowing from the throne of God and of the Lamb.

'Just a Reminder-Each Day'

Opportunities

I consider myself to be a privileged person. My mother looked for opportunities to improve my horse-riding skills. On one such occasion, she took a friend and me to the city to a five-day riding school. The instructors were highly recommended. Some came from Europe to share their horsemanship in Australia.

Setting up in the Park Lands each day, parents and friends would sit on their deck chairs and watch 20 to 30 young riders undergo some intense training. The exciting part was how each one of us improved. Through good instruction, we accomplished so much more than we had dreamed of. Our dressage and show jumping improved quite noticeably. It was a wonderful opportunity that greatly benefitted my friend and me. Looking back on my childhood, I am reminded of the many times my mother took someone else's child to similar events. She was not the only person who did those favours. I see parents today who happily offer to take other parents' children to sports, camps, and youth events. The good side of society takes care of those who can't do as much for themselves and their children. It is commendable.

As Christians, I wonder if we realise how valuable it is to help others, adults and children, hear about Jesus. Inviting or offering a ride to people to listen to a visiting evangelist, joining us at church or Bible study or attending a camp can make a big difference for those who otherwise couldn't attend these events. Jesus always seemed to have a huge following. I wonder if people invited each other to hear him.

"Lord God, thank you for all of life's great opportunities. Please help us to know when and whom to invite. Thank you, Jesus."

Luke 14: 13,14
(Then Jesus said to his host) "But when you give a banquet, invite the poor, the crippled, the lame, the blind, and you will be blessed. Although they cannot repay you, you will be repaid at the resurrection of the righteous."

January 14
Shame

Sometimes, I feel so sorry when I remember the things I am ashamed of. There are times when I let people down, am too selfish to care for others, fail to be supportive, choose myself before others, make a fool of myself, try too hard to get the attention of others, speak out of turn, and the list goes on. I could not write the stories of my shameful acts for others to read. Simply, I would be too ashamed.

Shame has two things in its favour; firstly, it reminds us of where we have gone wrong, and secondly, it reminds us to find a way to correct those mistakes. It is vitally important to control our feelings of shame and to take them to God. In taking our shame to God, we can ask for his forgiveness and help in forgiving ourselves. Suffering from shame puts us in a vulnerable position. If we do not take it to God, it can become a weapon in the Devil's hands to accuse and torment us. Don't let the Devil get started.

God forgives and repairs us but the devil keeps accusing us. God's weapon for defence is the Name of Jesus. The Bible tells us to stand firm against the devil with the full armour of God. (Ephesians 6) It doesn't matter how eloquently we pray or how awkwardly; once we have told the devil to go in Jesus' Name, we have tapped into untold power. God does the rest. If you need to apply the power of God to your situation, please pray this prayer aloud to put an end to feeling ashamed.

"Father God, I ask for your forgiveness for..................and the power to leave my shame behind."

"In the name of Jesus, I am no longer guilty of/ a victim of............ because I have his forgiveness. Get away from me Satan; in Jesus' Name, you can no longer accuse me of something God has already forgiven me of."

"Lord God, you are my hope in desperate times. No one can set me free like you. Thank you, Jesus."

1 Peter 5: 8,9
Be self-controlled and alert. Your enemy the devil prowls around like a roaring lion looking for someone to devour. Resist him, standing firm in your faith-

January 15

Polocrosse

The goal shooter for the Blues snatched the ball out of the air, galloped down the field on his horse, bounced the ball over the 30-yard line, and threw a goal unopposed. All the players cantered back to the throw-in, and before anyone else could get their racquet to the ball, Dave caught it again, galloped down to his goal-throwing area, and threw another goal. Gradually, the opposition realised they must try to stop the master at his game, But in record time, the ball was trapped in mid-air and another goal was thrown. Dave lines up again with his team members behind him and the opposition jostling for a better position. The umpire blows the whistle, throws the ball in and with a flick of his polocrosse stick, the ball lands in Dave's possession again! The rest is history.

In the 8-minute chukka, this brilliant horseman threw eight goals. That remarkable display of polocrosse was talked about for quite a while after that Grand Final game.

Outstanding achievements become everyone's story; even the opposition will acknowledge the event. When the Israelites went to war against their enemies, God gave them exceptional victory. Even the defeated nations talked about God.

When God is on our side, we can have confidence in his support.

"Lord God, I thank you for the thrill of watching polocrosse and other sports where people display exceptional skills. Please help us to see the

victories you win for us and help us to celebrate your greatness. Thank you, Jesus."

Isaiah 12: 4
In that day you will say, "Give praise to the Lord, proclaim his name; make known among the nations what he has done, and proclaim that his name is exalted."

Hopping Away

You don't have to live too far from an Australian city to have a kangaroo story to tell. This unique animal comes out of its home in a paddock or scrub to cross a busy road, often at the wrong time. Motorists will do their best to avoid hitting a kangaroo because, as well as injuring the animal, cars can be badly damaged, too.

Enjoying coffee on the veranda of a country shop with family and friends, I was surprised to see a lady approaching with a joey cradled in her arms. The young kangaroo was wrapped in a blanket with its head peeping out and calmly viewing its surroundings. I quickly reached down to make sure our dog was secured to the veranda post, as the smell of a kangaroo often gets a dog way too excited. We talked to the lady and then went on our way. No drama.

The next day, at the beach, the dog and I were swimming with family and friends. Our dog was confidently swimming quite a distance from me, unleashed and out quite deep. I saw the lady with the kangaroo wander down to the beach. She waded into the water with the joey still cradled in her arms. I called our dog to my side. She obediently swam beside me and out of the water. I was glad to get her on a lead and into my husband's care. Only just in time, it seemed. As the lady let her kangaroo down for a hop around, the youngster took fright. It leapt from the shallow sea, across the sand, up into the car park and out of sight, with the lady in hot pursuit. Our dog was tugging hard at her lead and shaking all over as she watched the kangaroo hop away.

Days later, I realised how badly that event could have ended. If our excited sheepdog, who thinks she is a kangaroo dog, had been free to chase the frightened animal, I'm sure we would not have been able to call her back.

"Lord God, thank you for stepping in and preventing disasters in our lives. Thank you for reminding us each day to pray for your guidance and protection over our activities and the adventures of our pets. Thank you, Jesus."

1 John 5: 14
This is the confidence we have in approaching God; that if we ask anything according to his will, he hears us and if we know that he hears us – whatever we ask – we know that we have what we asked for.

'Just a Reminder-Each Day'

Attention to Detail

Walking along one of the back streets in our small country town, my attention was drawn to some plants in a wine barrel. White flowers filled the barrel to the point of overflowing. It was an eye-catching display. Some people are very clever at decorating and making something look special. Artistic girls doodle on their notebooks and young men decorate their utilities. The gateways on some properties are big and extravagant. People who exhibit their show animals wash, trim, comb and decorate them beyond belief. Some homes are adorned with many ornaments. Special occasions, weddings, birthday parties, conventions and visits by dignitaries allow the opportunity to give attention to detail. Flower arrangements, balloons, draped fabric and carpet rolled out tell us how important the event is. In the book of Exodus, we are given an example of how pedantic one can be about detail. Blue, purple and scarlet yarn were woven together, gold braiding, and every precious stone you could think of was sewn into garments for the priests to wear while worshipping God. The Israelites had been through tough times, but this new era of doing everything with pageantry, and with so much attention to detail, was all about celebrating God in gratitude. We may question why God instructed Moses to spend so much money and time creating these garments and accessories while employing the best craftsmen for their workmanship. Still, he was making a statement that is relevant to us today. Worship God, be grateful to him and give attention to detail to announce the importance of God.

When planning our youth events, someone often wants to splash colour around, decorating the venue with streamers and balloons in line with the theme. The effort put in demonstrates how important we feel the event is. We want those attending to find out how important God is.

"Lord God, we realise we get a little complacent about having you as our God. Please help us get excited and celebrate your goodness with enthusiasm. Thank you, Jesus."

Exodus 39: 25
And they made bells of pure gold and attached them around the hem between the pomegranates. The bells and pomegranates alternated around the hem of the robe to be worn for ministering as the Lord commanded Moses.

January 18

Remember When

Squeals of delight echoed along the wharf. Small children jumped into the deep sea, their small frames paddling back to the steps just to repeat the jump all over again. Some of the smallest children had life jackets on and when they hit the water, their upper bodies didn't even submerge. There was hardly a hint of wind, the sun was warm but not hot and parents hovered around with one eye on their fishing rod and the other on their adventurous children. I sat on a moderately comfortable concrete seat with my favourite person in life while allowing the tranquillity of the moment to engulf me. I was back on home territory, and it was no effort to recall what it felt like to be a child in a group of excited children preparing for the next big jump.

The next day, at home, I thought about our time at Port Vincent and I felt good, as you do when you reflect on a happy event.

Today, we are more aware of the unhappy events that cause us stress and anxiety. The media ensures we know all the gory details of violence, war, poverty and natural disasters. Our minds are given a lot to process, more than is healthy for us. As a result, we either become hardened, find ways to help, or let it get us down. For a good balance in our lives, we need to allow the Holy Spirit to filter what we hear and see. Knowing when to take it seriously and when to leave what we can't change is helpful. Positive, happy events and thoughts are good for reflection. They can give us peace and gratitude.

The other side of this dilemma is our desire to be helpful in some of the hardest situations. Some people are real heroes in the way they give so much of themselves to helping others, but they need some form of inner strength to survive.

We all need inner peace and faith to hold us together. God is the support we need whether we stay out of stressful situations or whether we become involved.

"Lord God, thank you for the good memories that lift our spirits and take us away from our anxious thoughts. Please equip us for the stressful situations we must cope with and those we choose to help in. Thank you, Jesus."

Philippians 4: 7
And the peace of God, which transcends all understanding will guard your hearts and your minds in Christ Jesus.

'Just a Reminder-Each Day'

Weather Events

Sheets of water lay all over the caravan park. Clothes on the line under our awning continued to drip and not dry. The dog decided that under such conditions, she must go under the caravan and just wait.

For those of us living in the driest state in our country, significant rain events in summer are most unusual. Rain is usually welcome, but after a while, it can become too much! Country people compare rain-fall tallies with each other. Weather events become the main topic of conversation. They talk about north winds and the danger of fires, but conversations about floods are rare. Then the question arises; "Where is God in all this?" Has God caused this weather event? Is he in the wind and rain? Does he have a good purpose in all of this? The rain continues and the rain-water tanks fill. The ground soaks up the mois-ture like a sponge, leaves on trees sparkle with dampness and small plants peep through the once hard soil.Days later, news reaches us of trucks bogged on their journey to take food to remote places and a friend's house being destroyed by gale-force winds. Again, we ask, "Where is God in all of this?" Like most people, I am not sure, but we know our God never leaves us and we must choose to trust him for our peace.

"Lord God, thank you for the wonderful rain that blesses our dry ground so much in summer. We ask for your comfort and healing for people who

have had property damage through floods, fires, and other dangerous weather events. Thank you, Jesus."

Isaiah 46: 4
Even to your old age and grey hairs I am he, I am he who will sustain you. I have made you and I will carry you; I will sustain you and I will rescue you.

Feeling at Home

A huge fire in the hills surrounding the city of Perth threatened a riding school where many horses were stabled. The owner of a horse transport was able to move the horses and ponies to another stable complex out of the path of the fire. Weeks after the danger had passed, a television program filmed the loading of the horses and ponies onto the transport to return them to their home. Some of the horses were nervous about walking into the truck, but an interesting phenomenon took place when they were returned to their home stable. Being led out of the truck by the transport owners, many ponies held their heads high and tense, looking around at a scenery they hadn't seen for weeks. As each one was handed over to their owners, most being young school-age girls, the ponies, as if sensing immediately they were with someone familiar, lowered their heads and walked alongside their little owners in a state of total peace. The transformation was lovely to watch.

Later, when I thought about the event I had watched on television, it reminded me of how uncomfortable I felt when I first started attending church. I was 22 years old and had only been to a few church services I could remember.

After I married, church attendance became a regular event, but I continued to feel uncomfortable. I felt I didn't belong and this went on for years. Even now, I realise that some church services continue to be far different from any other community event outside the church.

The real difference now is how I feel in my relationship with God who should be the focal point of church services. Knowing and experiencing His Spirit within me has given me confidence in being a part of the church community. I think we need to be honest as Christians and allow others to see our vulnerability, sharing our highs and lows and acknowledging God as our strength. Bible study in our home and that of friends has been a positive experience and made it much easier for me to feel accepted. Less formality and the lack of tradition seem helpful.

"Lord God, please help us empathise with others outside the church who just need to be accepted. Thank you, Jesus."

Psalm 13: 5
But I trust in your unfailing love; my heart rejoices in your salvation. I will sing to the Lord because he has been good to me.

'Just a Reminder-Each Day'

Aspiring to Be Great

Many people dream of making it to the big stage. Modern technology and communication have enabled those with little resources to tap into the same support as those with all they need. Athletes can view the human body in action on a screen, in slow motion, sinew by sinew, to copy great styles. The internet can equip people with knowledge, methods, and shortcuts to success. There are coaches, motivational speakers and finance available to help people climb the ladder of success like never before. It is much easier now to achieve greatness than decades ago. I could even arrange a vase of flowers by watching a YouTube clip – maybe!

The life Jesus lived was exemplary. The places he went, the types of people he associated with, the miracles he performed, the wise words he spoke and the insight he had, set him apart from all other men of his time and even now he is revered by 31 % of the world's population, 2.383 billion people.

Some people tried to copy him but their fraudulent behaviour let them down. While Jesus was teaching and equipping his followers, many went out converting and healing in his name. Jesus had the power to be great and he certainly had the big stage to stand on, with crowds following him from town to town. He empowered some of his followers to do the same things he was doing.

There is nothing wrong with aspiring to do great things, but as Christians, we are better off realising who is empowering us and how to make it to the big stage, his way, if he sees fit.

"Lord God, thank you for the determination and drive we have that makes us want to be great. Please direct our thoughts, actions and dreams into your hands. Please help us to achieve our goals, acknowledging our dependence on you. Thank you, Jesus."

John 15: 5
Jesus said, "I am the vine; you are the branches. If a man remains in me and I in him, he will bear much fruit; apart from me you can do nothing."

'Just a Reminder-Each Day'

Fingernails

After a week at the beach, I realised the holiday had been kind to my fingernails, too. They had grown! I have very poor nails, some fault lines that split easily, and generally, the whole nail angles away from my fingers, sticking up and asking for trouble. Gardening, horse riding and most other physical activities are bad for my nails. They are usually in some sort of disrepair. I believe this is not just my problem; others have similar trouble, too. It would be

nice if we could go through life preserving our bodies from harm, but the satisfaction and sense of achievement that comes from physical work, even if it is just for pleasure, is hard to beat. Physical activity is a healthy, good-for-us part of life.

Modern technology has changed the look of work. The original hard labour jobs are now done with big equipment, especially for those of us living in the Western world. Working from a computer is probably the most significant change in how people work since the horse-drawn ploughs changed to tractor-powered.

"Lord God, help us to be able to work according to our ability and enjoyment. Please open opportunities for work in areas that will most benefit us and those dependent on us. Please help us to know what the best lifestyle is for us, the amount of work we should do and not do and where we can volunteer or receive help. Thank you, Jesus."

1 Thessalonians 4: 11
Make it your ambition to lead a quiet life, to mind your own business and to work with your hands, just as we told you, so that your daily life may win the respect of outsiders and so that you will not be dependent on anybody.

Drifting

Our four-wheel drive, Red Patrol became a popular vehicle to train young people to drive. Its smooth gearbox made for easy gear changes and its elevated seats enabled even short drivers to see where they were going, although reaching the clutch and accelerator pedal was challenging for some. No one ever complained when they were invited to have a drive. The farm, with its flat, uninterrupted pasture paddocks, made a safe environment for beginners.

One day, I had our eldest granddaughter in the driver's seat. She was concentrating hard on doing a good job, but her cheeky Uncle came along on his motorbike and rode beside us for a while. When she noticed him, she began to drift his way. She seemed to be using him as a guide to drive straight. Her Uncle had a big grin on his face as he became aware that she had lost her focus on following the track home. By then, her mother who was sitting in the back seat, and I were laughing quietly to ourselves. The further our driver drifted towards the motorbike, the further her uncle moved into the centre of the paddock. It must have looked funny, but our eleven-year-old granddaughter thought she was going fine so long as she kept a healthy distance from the motorbike. What she did not realise was that she was getting way off course. Eventually, I decided to correct the vehicle by taking hold of the steering wheel and guiding it back onto the track.

She accepted the correction without a word and refocused on the drive home.

I don't know how many times in life we drift away from the track that leads us directly to what is best for us and how often God reaches over and brings us back on course. If we have made it clear to God that we want and respect his guiding hand in our lives, we can expect to have it.

Our granddaughter has grown up proving to be a very reliable driver.

"Lord God, thank you for being so invested in our lives that you are willing to bring us back on track. Please continue to guide the way we live. Thank you, Jesus."

Proverbs 4: 25-27
Let your eyes look straight ahead, fix your gaze directly before you. Make level paths for your feet and take only ways that are firm. Do not swerve to the right or the left; keep your foot from evil.

January 24
Retaliate

Returning from my early morning walk with the dog, I could see a man approaching, leading two medium-sized black dogs. The man hesitated when he realised we would pass each other through a narrow part of the caravan park; he checked his dogs and proceeded. His actions gave me a little warning, but I continued. My dog was doing well; she was focused on returning to the caravan, walking straight and seemingly uninterested in the approaching dogs. I continued in confidence. I looked at the man as we got close enough for eye contact, expecting to exchange a 'good morning', but it was soon clear that he had other things on his mind when one of his dogs lurched towards my dog. "Here, Bella," the man called as he tugged his dog back into line. To my disappointment, my dog retaliated.

Dogs react so quickly; no wonder we owners get into trouble some-times. I grabbed a shorter hold of her lead and pulled her back to my side as we continued our walk.

As much as I want my dog to avoid reacting when something threatens her and to trust me to manage the situation, I know that won't always work. I also know we humans are prone to retaliate, too. We all too easily lose our self-control when we disagree, speak out of turn when we feel opposed and jump to our defence and that of family and friends when we feel threatened. It is as if we are on our own in life's challenges, instead of looking to God and his Spirit who is our defence.

"Lord God, I admit to retaliating all too often. Please help me to have self-control and to turn to you who can defend me better than I can defend myself. Thank you, Jesus."

Ecclesiastes 7: 9
Do not be quickly provoked in your spirit, for anger resides in the lap of fools.

‘Just a Reminder-Each Day’

Organised

Our son, his wife and four young daughters were going on holiday. I had a parcel to go with them. "We'll be leaving early," my son warned me. When we met them along the road it was quite a sight. Their station wagon was packed high with bedding, clothes, food and fishing rods. Four sleepy little heads peeped out at us from a sea of quilts and pillows as we passed our parcel to them. The girls were still in their pyjamas and were expected to sleep a little longer before the sun rose. The plan was that the seven-hour-long trip to the shack would be better managed if the children could sleep for part of it.

Living where we live, we often see cars piled high with holiday gear crammed in and on top of their vehicles. Some people can be

prepared well before their departure time, enabling them to arrive at their holiday destination in daylight, but not all people are that well organised.

Anxiety and impatience seem to go with planning for big events, but the Holy Spirit offers comfort and self-control. It is nice to have God's help at these times.

"Lord God, we are always planning something, whether it is a big holiday or a daily task. Please direct our thinking and help us to plan wisely, acknowledging you in all our plans. Thank you, Jesus."

Proverbs 14: 22b
Those who plan what is good find love and faithfulness.

Red Hatters

I hope you are ready for a laugh today!

Walking across the caravan park from our van to the amenities, I approached a woman who was representing her generation by the clothes she was wearing – black shorts, a black top – thongs (the ones with a bit of class), and her blonde hair piled on top of her head. We greeted each other with "Good morning" and continued in opposite directions. I wondered what her summary was of me. I was wearing my pink shorts, a colour I find hard to tastefully match, a purple polo shirt, my zip-up rusty red windcheater and a pair of red socks, a Christmas present from my grandson, and my white sneakers with purple trim!

I'm sure having a good laugh is good for us. I will be disappointed when I see the Lord face to face and find I have missed too many opportunities to laugh. The whole of creation has so many quirky, funny things to appreciate and laugh at. People can be funny just by being themselves. It's good to laugh without offending, laugh for pleasure, laugh at animal antics and children innocently attempting impossible things. Some people are clever at making us laugh.

At a youth camp, one person read out a very funny story that uses numbers to replace words intermittently and when read out aloud, it is clever and hilarious. When he had finished reading, I stood up to announce the next item but the minute I opened my mouth, I started laughing uncontrollably. I was useless! As a result, the audience began laughing at me! Contagious laughter does us good, too.

I have a friend who has joined a group of ladies called the 'Red Hatters'. Established in America in 1998, this organisation chooses to dress up in red hats teamed with purple attire. They use it as an excuse to catch a little attention, a reason to laugh, to go out together for meals and conventions and to join in any other suitable celebrations. Their motto is Live, Love, Laugh.

"Lord God, thank you for laughter, for the excuse to focus on something amusing. Thank you for the people around us who permit us to laugh, those who use their sense of humour to entertain us. Thank you, Jesus."

Proverbs 15: 30
A cheerful look brings joy to the heart, and good news gives health to the bones.

January 27

Blame Game

Denying our responsibility sets up an obstacle in the way of us reaching our full potential. When we see politicians playing the Blame Game, saying it is the other side's fault, it is a bit hard to take. Children often play the blame game, but for some, it continues into adulthood. People lose credibility if they keep blaming others. We look for truth in the people who lead us, whether in the government, the medical system, church, schools or sport, to name a few.

When I was at a Pony Club camp in my very early teens, a group of us older campers got into trouble. We had been misbehaving. When it came to admitting what we had done wrong, I refused to, and instead, I was happy to blame the other group of campers. It was wrong for me to do that, and I'm ashamed of my actions as the rest of my group apologised for what they did. If I had apologised straight away, it would have all been forgotten and never thought of again, but my irresponsible action means I still think of it and feel remorseful. It's too late to correct it now except to apologise to the Lord, which I have done. I appreciate the forgiveness promised to us by God.

"Lord God, we know you like honesty and accountability. Please forgive us for the mistakes we have made. Please help us avoid the blame game, but instead choose to walk in truth and honesty. We pray for our government, leaders and world powers, asking you to keep them honest and avoid blaming others. Thank you, Jesus."

Acts 13: 38,39

Therefore friends, I want you to know that through Jesus the forgiveness of sins is proclaimed to you. Through him everyone who believes is set free from every sin, a justification you were not able to obtain under the law of Moses.

'Just a Reminder-Each Day'

January 28
Not Clever at School

We all hear stories of how young boys behave in their school years. They get labelled as disruptive, inattentive, and easily bored while girls are usually happier and more studious. Generally, girls write neater, take pride in their work and relate well to each other, while some boys are hard to motivate. However, we also know that some of those boys have grown up to be real achievers, good businessmen and leaders in society.

I struggled with school most of the time. My spelling was poor, and I was only marginally good at maths.

My poor achievement at school has been an embarrassment in my adult life. Some changes took place when I became a Christian. God gave me the desire to read the Bible. Reading previously had been a struggle. The Bible became easy to read! I enjoyed it and I looked forward to getting revelations from reading it. Then, on a small scale, I went into sharing my faith and understanding of God with others.

God has a plan even for people like me. God took me in hand and enabled me to do things academically I never dreamt of. We should never put ourselves down because God can miraculously lift us up to a more useful and satisfying place.

"Lord God, you knew us before we were born. You know our weaknesses and our strengths. You have a good plan for each one of us. Please help those of us who struggle academically. Please enable us, by the power

of your Holy Spirit, to achieve in the areas we find difficult. Thank you, Jesus."

Philippians 4: 19
And my God will meet all your needs according to his glorious riches in Christ Jesus.

 "

When the Threat is Over

As we walked out the door of our local doctor's Surgery I realised the information we had been given after our coronavirus vaccination booster went further than informing me. It managed to lay a threat on me. 'Five to seven days and you'll know if you are going to have any heart problems' was the advice given to us. In the ten minutes after the vaccination, my heart had started to race, so I was already feeling a little uneasy.

I sipped my coffee and gazed out the caravan door, thoroughly enjoying our seaside holiday. We had packed drinks, sunscreen, and snacks for another day at the beach with our daughter, the grandchildren and all their friends. Then, it dawned on me that it was day eight since we had received our booster vaccine. The threat was over! I admit that I had hardly thought much about it. We had prayed for God's protection, packed for our holiday, driven for a day and finally settled into the holiday atmosphere at our usual destination. We hadn't been waiting for the seven days to be over, on the contrary, we were carried along by the change of venue and the whole holiday experience. It would be nice if we could always leave our worries behind and go on holidays, but I like to think that praying for God's protection plays a big part in our peace, not just the holiday.

"Lord God, thank you for the liberating feeling we get when you lift burdens from our lives. Please help us to put future concerns in your hands and trust you for the outcome. Thank you, Jesus."

2 Corinthians 3: 17
Now the Lord is the Spirit, and where the Spirit of the Lord is, there is freedom.

'Just a Reminder-Each Day'

January 30
Mirror

'**M**irror, mirror on the wall, who is the fairest of them all?' I remember that line distinctly from the children's book 'Snow White and the Seven Dwarfs'. We, too, use the mirror to judge how fair or good-looking we are. We do not like to admit that we give the mirror too much of our time, but it does seem to have some power over us.

So many things seem unclear as a child, but they become clearer when we reach adulthood – so it is with our understanding and concept of God that it will become clearer. Without looking in a mirror, peering into clear water or seeing

our reflection in a shop window we would not know what we look like. Thanks to the all-too-revealing mirror, we know exactly what we look like. The mirror reflects us as we are, no matter how hard we try to change our looks. It is hard to let go of our mirror image, but it seems far more valuable for us to reflect God than to worry about what we look like.

"Lord God, please help us to see ourselves as you see us rather than worry about the image we reflect. Thank you, Jesus."

1 John 3: 1,2b
How great is the love the Father has lavished on us, that we should be called children of God! But we know that when he appears, we shall be like him, for we shall see him as he is.

January 31
My Testimony

My story starts in a small country town hall where a group of people, including a nine-year-old boy from another church, came to share their faith. I was tired but on a high as we had just arrived home from running our annual Pony Club Camp. All through my teen years, this had been the highlight of my year. I don't remember what was said that night, but I guess it was all about Jesus. My friend, who also helped us run the PC camp, was in tears at the end of the talks. I felt emotional, too, but I put it down to being tired from running the camp. When I went to bed that night, I felt some pressure in my spirit to make a decision! Almost irritably, I said privately to God, "I give up. You can have my life!" At that, I went to sleep. The next morning, I realised I had a new job to tackle. As a newlywed farmer's wife, I had never had to cater for shearers before. I knew there was an unwritten law that all smokos and lunches had to be on time! As I prepared the food, I realised I was now a Christian and ought to be able to ask God to help me, so out loud, I asked for his guidance on every aspect of preparing the food. The more I asked, the more it seemed only fitting to do so, and I gained the confidence to request more. I was still very nervous about supplying a meal for men I didn't know in my small, awkward kitchen but I felt the prayer helped.

I knew nothing about God or had ever attended a church until I started dating Phil, the man I married. God had brought me into a Christian family and, even better, onto the doorstep of revival. My point of conversion was like stepping into a brand-new world; it was like going from the unknown to the known. From that night on, I understood and believed in God with hardly a doubt.

In my journey as a Christian, I have struggled hugely over whether I should give up riding horses to serve God. One thing I understand better now is that serving means doing life with the Holy Spirit in everything we do and anywhere we go, and it should be fun and fulfilling.

"Lord God, thank you for the greatest gift of all, faith in you. Thank you, Jesus."

Romans 10: 9
That if you confess with your mouth, "Jesus is Lord," and believe in your heart that God raised him from the dead, you will be saved.

Ice Cold Reception

I walked up to the desk. The lady seated on the other side looked up from her work and stared at me. I presented my question, hoping she could direct me to the kind of book I was looking for. Her gaze never changed. Her hard, cold expression was fixed on me. I was starting to feel intimidated, so I quickly rephrased my question and made it sound more sophisticated; and more educated! Still, she stared, and I felt panicky as I tried a little humour. Then, as if she swapped out of whatever was holding her captive, she asked me a question. I had been wondering if my first question had her thinking deeply about where that kind of book might be or if they even had any. A heap of excuses for her behaviour flooded my mind; 'I must look too dumb to be purchasing that kind of book', 'She must know I'm a country woman in the city, and I'm obviously not cool'.

By now, I was really wishing I had not gone into her shop or at least she would say they didn't have the book and then I could run out, feeling sorry for myself.

The awkward relationship was not going to end that neatly. The lady had walked off and came back with a few books that might be what I wanted. Instead of feeling grateful, I quickly flicked through the books on the counter where she had placed them and made a too-hasty decision. I was quite glad to get out of that shop.

I've grown in confidence and have learned to listen to the Holy Spirit more since then. I know I need to stay calm and try to pray for people rather than judge them. It isn't easy, but with God's help it can turn out better.

"Lord God, please help us to be discerning and able to keep in perspective what is happening around us. Thank you, Jesus."

1 Peter 4: 7,8
Therefore, be clear-minded and self-controlled so that you can pray. Above all, love each other deeply, because love covers a multitude of sins.

February 2
Elijah-Risk Taker

When the prophet Elijah spoke to King Ahab about some bad stuff that was going to happen, he feared for his life. God sent him first to a cave to hide where the ravens would feed him with bread and meat in the morning and evening. God told him he could drink from a nearby brook each day. From that point on, God arranged places to shelter and protect Elijah until the danger was over, but it was not always fun! When the brook dried up, God arranged for a widow in Zarephath to care for him. After Elijah arrived at her home, she announced to him that she and her son only had enough food left for their final meal. Elijah reassured her that her supply of flour would not run out nor her jar of oil, so the three of them managed until another bad situation arose; the widow's son died. God raised the boy back to life through the pleading prayers of Elijah. He was saved again!

The statement that the widow made to Elijah, announcing her faith in God, reminds us that in all our attempts to be God's messengers, the journey and the results are in his hands. Our reward is hearing people admit to understanding God and recognising that he is the truth.

"Lord God, please give us the courage to be your messenger, to take risks and trust you to take care of us along the way. Thank you, Jesus."

The prophet Elijah said to King Ahab, "As the Lord, the God of Israel, lives, whom I serve, there will be neither dew nor rain in the next few years except at my word."

Then the woman said to Elijah, "Now I know that you are a man of God and that the word of the Lord from your mouth is the truth,"

'Just a Reminder-Each Day'

February 3

Amazing

Our earthly life gives us many experiences and being amazed is one of them. Being amazed is almost a spiritual experience.

A delightful video that made it to the top of a television program featuring funny home videos, was of a little girl blowing the candles out on her birthday cake. Her face lit up with sheer amazement as she blew each candle out, one by one. Between blows, she would reflect, lean back in her highchair, and then blow again until all three were out. The joy on her face, as the final candle responded to her inexperienced blowing, was captivating. It was so funny and heart-warming to watch.

The privilege of watching children do things for the first time can be amazing. Unexpected antics by pets like a cat stalking itself in a mirror, special accomplishments by athletes, the coming together of two people who seem an unlikely match and magical sunsets add to our experience of being amazed. They are usually 'feel good' experiences.

The crowds following Jesus around had reason to be amazed, too, just as we would be today if someone were healing sick people, telling intriguing parables and walking on water. To have been in the presence of a man who could calm the sea, multiply food, turn water into wine and heal a paralysed man would have been a spiritual experience of amazement.

"Lord God, thank you for all the amazing things you have shown and continue to show us. Help us recognise you in our earthly experiences, the joy and amazement of driving a harvesting machine or watching a child take its first steps. Thank you for these faith-building, amazing moments in our lives. Open our eyes to see that it is you who performs the amazing. Thank you, Jesus".

Luke 5:17,24, 26
And the power of the Lord was present for him to heal the sick.
   He said to the paralysed man, "I tell you, get up, take your mat and go home."
   Everyone was amazed and gave praise to God. They were filled with awe and said, "We have seen remarkable things today."

Broken Can't be Fixed

After my husband and I were married, the question was often put to me by well-meaning people. "What was your maiden name?" "Who were you before you were married?" or "Who are your parents?"

I found the questions very embarrassing, and my husband understood why. My parents split up when I was young, and my mother's second marriage failed. I didn't know which name would be a satisfactory answer. My biological father was living interstate and my stepfather wasn't someone I wanted to be associated with. It was awkward and embarrassing each time someone asked me those questions.

It was less common for parents to split up when I was a child, but decades later, it has become much more common. We may assume, then, that children are less affected today.

Not at all! Children are hurt, bruised, confused and saddened. Some struggle to find something normal to hang onto. Life for them is never going to be the same. It doesn't matter whose fault it is that the marriage has failed; the children still suffer. Most break-ups don't mend. Children are left to adapt. They don't have a voice or know how to articulate their feelings. Their hurt often shows up in actions, especially unacceptable behaviour.

Stability is what they need because stability is what they have lost. They need people who will not change or leave them. They need to know Jesus as a friend who can be talked to in their bedroom, while they are out riding their bike, playing sport or at school. Jesus is the approachable, totally understanding friend for broken children to turn to. Parents can help by printing a few simple, encouraging Bible verses to stick on their mirrors or put under their pillows. Playing Christian songs and hanging out with a Christian group can be a way of mending. Pray and pray again for hurting children. With God's help, broken people (even children) can be fixed!

"Lord God, I thank you for healing the hurts in my life and making me aware of those who need support. Please look after children who are victims of marriage break-ups. Thank you, Jesus."

Psalm 9:10
Those who know your name will trust in you, for you Lord, have never forsaken those who seek you.

Purposely Designed

Most of us would not call ourselves designers, but most of us design something at some stage. God has provided this earth with endless materials and mediums for designing. Fabric, flowers, paper, wood and steel materials come quickly to mind. Designing also plays a part in house building, gardens, town planning, machinery and cars, music, dance and entertainment, particularly with the use of computers.

So many areas of our lives are designed. All this is only possible because God first designed this world. He then designed men and women and gave them the ability to do their own designing. I love designing, but I'm not necessarily good at it, so my designs just stay in my little world. God created everything for his pleasure and then put it in our hands! Wow! What an honour to have his world to work with.

After the South Australian fires at Pinery in 2015, a farmer culti-vated his property in an eye-catching design. It was noticed by planes that flew over that area. Many people photographed it. Some thought his cultivating was just for fun but the design was done specifically to prevent the charred land from drifting. The Pinery fire was a tragic event with the loss of human life, homes, sheds, livestock, crops and trees. For as far as could be seen the land was bare ground. The farming community eventually found the courage to start again. The artistically cultivated paddocks were a sign that farmers would grow crops and raise stock again. So much more of God's unique design is seen by air. Rivers, lakes, forests, mountains and cloud formations can be stunning to view. We are all designers, even if it is just how we comb our hair daily.

"Lord God, thank you for the gift of design and the impact and interest it gives to our lives. Please help us to be creative as you are creative. Thank you, Jesus."

Isaiah 45:18
For this is what the Lord says – he who created the heavens, he is God; he who fashioned and made the earth, he founded it; he did not create it to be empty but formed it to be inhabited.

Teach a Young Person

I t is not hard to see which decade a person has grown up in. Our ability to use technology shows our age. The things we learn when we are young usually stay with us, but learning something new later in life is not so easy. The conversation between those over 50 is often about technology and how frustrating it is. Our children can keep in step with television, mobile phones and computers but do they have a good understanding of God?

Recent generations have been quietly slipping away from traditional church attendance. Some have aligned themselves with Pentecostal churches, but generally, the number of young people associated with church compared with the 1950s has seriously declined.

The attitude of some parents has been that their kids will automatically follow in their footsteps. They seem to think their children will know God without any specific teaching or discussion on matters of faith. I believe, as parents, we need to be transparent with our children or any young people we associate with. They need to see us taking our problems to the Lord. They learn by hearing us discuss God and openly praying for help and guidance. If we believe that God is central to our lives and we put our trust in him, we must teach our children that this can also work for them.

A family who reads the Bible and prays together is at least giving themselves a good chance of having faith that will sustain them. We need to pray for our children and be ready to answer their questions confidently, with no conditions. God's gift of salvation through faith in Jesus is freely available to us, and it must also be easily available to our children.

"Lord God, we ask for our children, grandchildren and the children we have cared for to know you and your salvation. Thank you, Jesus."

Proverbs 22:6
Train a child in the way he should go, and when he is old, he will not turn from it.

Psalm 71:17
Since my youth O God, you have taught me and to this day I declare your marvellous deeds.

'Just a Reminder-Each Day'

Repent like in Nineveh

In Matthew 12:38, Jesus refers to the story of Jonah and the whale and follows it up by accusing the people around him of being wicked and adulterous because, instead of repenting, they wanted to see miracles. When Jonah told the people of Nineveh that they had to shape up or in forty days they would be overthrown, they were scared and asked God for forgiveness. The Ninevites had slipped into some godless, immoral living. The good end to that story is how God forgave the people of Nineveh.

In our generation, wicked and adulterous behaviour is often subtle, done secretly and covered up by a modern justification of an old law. We accept adultery as just an affair and deviating from the Biblical outline of marriage is seen as all right. Turning our back on God has allowed society to indulge in many other activities that used to be immoral and unacceptable. Opposing this behaviour sometimes gets us labelled as old-fashioned, not moving forward or interfering with people's freedoms.

When Jesus was talking to the crowds and referring to Jonah, he told them that one greater than Jonah was with them. The importance of recognising Jesus as God had escaped them. They were not getting it! God was standing right in front of them in the person of Jesus. Like the people in Nineveh, they should have been shaking in their boots and asking for forgiveness. From reading about the rest of Jesus' time on earth, we know many did repent and honour him as God, but it took a while.

The Holy Spirit has a way of showing us where we are going wrong while helping us to make the right changes. Many people have a strong conviction to change society and reset our moral compass.

"Lord God, please help us to see clearly how we should live for our good. Help us to fight off the urge to take an easy path that we may regret later. Thank you for your constant forgiveness that resets our course and frees us from condemnation. Help us to take a stand for right living and have the courage to make changes. Thank you, Jesus."

Proverbs 28: 14
Blessed is the man who always fears the Lord, but he who hardens his heart falls into trouble.

'Just a Reminder-Each Day'

Heaven Is

The conversation flowed as story after story was told. Near-death experiences, unpredicted events, angels, spiritual encounters and anything that shone a little light on the truth of heaven, were discussed. People added their ideas and no one professed to know what was real, but all agreed that you couldn't dispute someone's experience. The question of heaven and its reality kept the conversation going. Our curiosity about life and death, heaven and hell, kept us focused on God. It was stimulating conversation and good to discuss the mystery of God and his kingdom without arousing any opposing ideas. The story of the apostle Paul and his vision is worth reading, 2 Corinthians 12: 2 onwards.

In the book, 'Johnny Cash – The Redemption of an American Icon,' by Greg Lawrie, the account of Johnny's near-death experience gives us another glimpse of heaven. *'Cash described it as a safe and warm place that grew brighter and more beautiful with every moment. He began to drift to its very centre, feeling a sense of joy unlike any he'd ever experienced before.'*

Other people have recorded very similar experiences. Their stories line up, giving us a better understanding of heaven.

"Lord God, please help us to have confidence in your provision of life after death, your gift to us through Jesus. Please show us how to live without fearing the unknown but having the assurance that heaven is real. Thank you, Jesus."

Hebrews 9: 24
For Christ did not enter a man-made sanctuary that was only a copy of the true one; he entered Heaven itself, now to appear for us in God's presence.

Bird's Nest

A panel show on television caught my attention. I noticed a guest on the panel, a woman, who had a strange hairstyle. When I thought more about it I realised that the bird's nest style was quite popular, mostly with young women. After a bit more thought, not concentrating on what the lady was saying, I considered the bird's nest style only looked strange on her because very few women in her age group had chosen to support that fashion. More commonly, younger women, with their pretty faces and youthful mannerisms, wore the bird's nest hairstyle with flair.

I am just guessing what this style is called, but to me, it looks like a half-finished or poorly constructed bird nest, with sticks poking out from the centre of the nest in all directions! Maybe if you are a bird, you purposely do that to catch the young fledglings if they happen to wander too far from home!

There was obviously a lot of fiery discussion in the Corinthian church when this 'new' way of doing things got out of order. Rather like a bird's nest hairstyle going in all directions! Prophesying and speaking in tongues randomly must have been a real rabble. So, the apostle Paul spent quite some time writing strong letters to the Corinthians encouraging them to conduct their worship in an orderly way.

You may have noticed that birds' nests come in all shapes and styles. Some are very compact and others are loose but still orderly. Another group appear randomly put together, not unlike the lady's hairstyle.

I love change and people being brave enough to express their feelings and wear wild hairstyles without reservation, but order is good, too.

"Lord God, it is a very interesting world you have given us and even more interesting and exciting are the gifts of your Holy Spirit. Please help us to use those gifts wisely and with the intent to help others. Thank you, Jesus."

1 Corinthians 14: 12, 33
Since you are eager to have spiritual gifts, try to excel in gifts that build up the church. For God is not a God of disorder but of peace.

'Just a Reminder-Each Day'

February 10
Leadership

Whenever a big event is about to take place, you can be sure someone or a committee of people has worked through all the details and planned thoroughly. The success of the event depends on the planning. Some events have rehearsals and some just happen on the day. Some people are born to be organisers and others are followers and supporters. Each one needs the other. Leadership will only be successful if the supporters follow the plans. We may be born to be leaders but, first, we must learn to follow. For the Christian, good leadership comes from being a supporter and follower of our God. Jesus had many followers and many of them became leaders. Whatever role attracts us, success depends on how much we respect the leadership of God's Holy Spirit within us. It is not the size of the event that matters but the value of it that counts. We should embrace leadership as an opportunity to make a difference.

"Lord God, we thank you for whatever leadership ability we have. Please help us to have the courage to take on a greater role or to know that we are already in the role that is right for us. We thank you for our leaders in government, local organisations and essential services. Thank you, Jesus."

1 Corinthians 12: 27,31
Now you are the body of Christ, and each one of you is a part of it. And in the church God has appointed first of all apostles, second prophets, third teachers, then workers of miracles, also those having gifts of healing, those able to help others, those with gifts of administration, and those speaking in different kinds of tongues. But eagerly desire the greater gifts.

February 11
Peace I Leave with You

Some people have to hang on, and some have to let go.

Mental breakdowns happen to all kinds of people through all sorts of situations. In hindsight, I realise now at what point I went into overload. I was tricked into thinking I could do more. I had recovered so well from my former breakdown and it felt so good to be useful. I felt almost invincible, so I kept taking on more challenges. This time when I broke down, I was useless. All the projects went on hold. I barely maintained my role as a wife and mother. My husband had to step up. It was a hard time for all of us.

Our Primary school-age children never complained, but they must have been aware that their Mum wasn't coping too well. I had a huge amount of support from my husband.

At my lowest point, full of fear that I was losing my sanity, I was desperate for God to help me. We never sought medical help, never actually thought of it. We were ignorant of what help may have been available. We prayed together a lot and managed one day at a time. I knew one thing I should do was let go and trust God to keep me sane, but I couldn't. I chose to hang on. I found two Bible readings that held some power for me. I wrote them in big letters and stuck them on my bedroom wall. Sometimes I couldn't even read them. Lying in bed I would just look at them, but they had some kind of power that kept me from panicking.

"Lord God, I am truly grateful that you got me through a very difficult time in my life. Thank you for your peace which seems to be able to get right into our minds where disturbing thoughts erupt. Thank you, Jesus."
Psalm 94: 19 (Living Bible) Lord, when doubts fill my mind, when my heart is in turmoil, quiet me and give me renewed hope and cheer.

John 14:27
Peace I leave with you; my peace I give you. I do not give as the world gives. Do not let your hearts be troubled and do not be afraid.

'Just a Reminder-Each Day'

Undeserved Favour

After holidaying in our caravan and being careful how much water we used, the full rainwater tanks at home were like an undeserved favour. The heavens had opened while we were away. The rain gauge was full and the garden looked exceptionally grateful. New shoots were appearing on the trees, shrubs and rose bushes. It took me a while to realise I could run water without making sure I only used what I needed.

The salvation Jesus made available to us is certainly undeserved favour. We had a friend once who insisted on returning favours which made it awkward to ask for anything. We felt obligated to return the favour as soon as possible. A relationship between friends where favours are appreciated and a return favour doesn't have to be given, is a much more comfortable relationship.

We found ourselves in need of a favour very recently. When we asked another friend for help she was excited at the opportunity to do something for us. Undeserved favours often show up when someone is a victim of an unpredicted event. When we have nothing to offer in return but receive favours anyway, it is just like God's gift of love towards us.

"Lord God, it can be hard to believe you accept us unconditionally even when we know we don't measure up. Thank you for the undeserved favours you give us so freely. Thank you, Jesus."

Titus 3: 4-7

But when the kindness and love of God our Saviour appeared, he saved us, not because of righteous things we had done, but because of his mercy. He saved us through the washing of rebirth and renewal by his Holy Spirit, whom he poured out on us generously through Jesus Christ our Saviour, so that, having been justified by his grace, we might become heirs having the hope of eternal life.

'Just a Reminder-Each Day'

February 13
The Coloured Pencils

was frustrated! 'How could she let him give me coloured pencils for Christmas?' I understood that he was only nine years old and could only think like a nine-year-old, but surely, she could have explained to him how inappropriate the gift was. 'I'm way too old to get the same pleasure from pencils that I did when I was a child,' I declared, consoling myself.

God's plans are above ours. I certainly couldn't see the bigger picture. I didn't realise my life was about to take on a new look. I had become a Christian, but I was just taking it one day at a time and not trying to overthink where this spiritual change would take me. I didn't foresee the day when I would be hungry to know the Bible and to start underlining bible verses. I was about to discover things that I had no idea ever existed.

The coloured pencils would become my first experience of underlining bible verses that impressed me. I felt good about using the pencils that had sat unused for almost a year. It all fell into place. The gift wasn't inappropriate at all. Each day I would try and make time to read my Bible and underline more and more amazing verses.

"Lord God, I thank you for the exciting journey of learning so much from your written word. Thank you for the coloured pencils and those special verses that have shaped my life. Thank you, Jesus."

'Just a Reminder-Each Day'

My Valentine

It was a privilege to have a young horse-riding friend stay with us. She brought her two horses to the farm and enjoyed riding all over our property. One day we were riding our horses in a small work arena. We stopped and talked to each other and allowed our horses to relax.

As our conversation went on, we noticed her chestnut Arab horse step slightly closer to my horse. A bit later, my little part Andalusian grey mare took a step closer to the chestnut. Very discretely, both horses took another step closer until they were able to rub their necks on each other. Mildly amused at their behaviour, we did not restrain them. Our light conversation turned into laughter as we watched our two horses showing genuine affection for each other. They not only rubbed their necks on each other, but they moved their bodies closer until our stirrups clinked. It was such a funny moment.

Relationships between men and women, young and old and people trying to establish a new relationship, can be complex. Unlike animals, we have a conscience that reminds us that we may not receive a warm reception. So many thoughts crowd our minds like; who is watching, what will people think, will I be rejected or accepted, does she/he like me or even want anything to do with me? Forming new relationships isn't necessarily easy, regardless of age or gender. Those who have the confidence to make an honest approach, mindful of how the other person is feeling, usually receive the best reception, even if the relationship does not progress.

Asking the Holy Spirit to prepare us and the other person, for our encounter, can be a great help in all relationships, not only in finding a partner.

In the book of James, the writer directs us to come near to God. We are free to approach God at any time, and the best part is that his response will always be acceptance of us.

"Lord God, thank you for being as close as a prayer away. Please help us with our relationships, so that we might approach people with respect and want the best for them also. Thank you, Jesus."

James 4: 8
Come near to God and he will come near to you.

February 15

Draw the Line

Quite a lot of South Australian farmland has been over-cleared. The early settlers worked hard to make a living. They cleared scrub to plant cereal crops and made little profit. The next generation profited from the first generation's hard work. The sad part is that we do not know where to draw the line. Too many trees and natural scrub have been removed, which is detrimental to our ecosystem. Birds and other natural predators have vanished, leaving the farmers compelled to use more chemical sprays to kill off pests and diseases.

Many laws are being debated in our parliament about gender equality, discrimination against transgender people and religious freedom, so we need, more than ever, God's wisdom.

The same problem existed in the upholding of laws in biblical times. The church leaders were so set on following the laws set down by Moses that they did not know where to draw the line. They made sure people knew about tithing, but they wanted them to give a tenth of everything, down to the smallest detail.

Jesus comes on the scene and he points out the dangers of not knowing where to draw the line. He met the challenges set before him with grace and Godly wisdom when he declared, 'Give to Caesar what is due to Caesar', 'If your sheep falls into a pit on Sunday get it out, without labelling it as work' and 'Stop loading people down with burdens they can hardly carry while you don't lift a finger to help them'. *(Matthew 22:21, Matthew 12:11, Luke 11:46)*

"Lord God, please show us if we are taking something too far or not far enough. Please help us see the best way of minding our patch, serving our community, and upholding the standards that sit right with you. Thank you, Jesus."

Luke 11: 42
"Woe to you Pharisees, because you give God a tenth of your mint, rue and all other kinds of garden herbs, but you neglect justice and the love of God. You should have practised the latter without leaving the former undone".

Serenity

The firm damp sand, which had not long before said goodbye to the receding tide, stretched as far as my eyes could see. The clouds overhead filtered out the hot sun and the serenity of the moment led me to talk out loud to my Lord. A handful of people stood on the jetty casting a line, their eyes focussed dreamily into the water below, totally unaware of my prayer going heavenward.

I asked the Lord for something that I doubted he would do. It was a prayer of hope but not of certainty. It reminded me of the Serenity prayer written in 1932/33 by an American theologian, Reinhold Niebuhr. Apparently, his first writing of the prayer went like this; *Father, give us the courage to change what must be altered, Serenity to accept what cannot be helped, and the insight to know the one from the other.* The prayer was adopted and popularised by Alcoholics Anonymous in 1943. We are more familiar with this version; *God, grant me the Serenity to accept the things I cannot change. The courage to change the things I can and the wisdom to know the difference.*

I continued to pray my prayer, but subconsciously I wondered if he had any plans to do what I was asking of him. The serenity of the moment made it easy to pray; the closeness of God in the wonder of his creation was about as real as it ever gets.

"Lord God, I thank you for those special moments where you seem close. Please help us to leave the things that seem impossible to change

if they are causing us stress. Help us to trust you with life's most difficult situations and know your peace. Thank you, Jesus."

Psalm 6: 9
The Lord has heard my cry for mercy; the Lord accepts my prayer.

Presents

Walking around the kitchen in my dressing gown, still in my "Don't talk to me, I'm not awake yet," state, I reached for a coffee cup. I selected the one with a pattern of green eucalyptus leaves, which my daughter-in-law had given me. I love the cup. My mind drifted to other presents that I hold in high regard; A jacket that came from our Japanese friend in Tokyo years ago, which seems to be a fashion item in Australia now, I wear it often. I thought about the two Bibles that have impacted my life significantly. The first Bible I was given was a Living Translation that was so easy to read, and later, the NIV, which is my constant companion while writing these articles. Last night seemed a bit cold, so I grabbed a blanket to add to our bed, subconsciously thanking Debbie for such a handy present.

Some presents have a way of automatically connecting us with the giver. Places and times have ways of connecting us, too. For some people, the desire to continue a relationship with a loved one who has died can be emotionally distressing. Photos take us back to events and people; sometimes the connection is very strong.

Jesus pointed out the benefits of having a connection with his Spirit and how that would work for his followers and for us, too. His Spirit joins us with God the Father and it also joins us with people. When I talk and listen to the Holy Spirit, I am in a relationship with God, who is also in a relationship with people in heaven, like my parents and friends who have died. I have confidence in His care for those I can no longer relate to, and that comforts me.

"Lord God, we thank you for the people who play an important part in our lives and for those we used to have a connection with. Please help us to have confidence in eternity and your Holy Spirit, who keeps us connected. Thank you, Jesus."

John 14: 16,17
(Jesus said) "And I will ask the Father, and he will give you another Counsellor to be with you for ever – the Spirit of truth. The world cannot accept him, because it neither sees him nor knows him. But you know him; he lives with you and will be in you."

Ice Cream

have never known a time when I could not have ice cream. It was an exciting day when my mother would announce that we would go to the delicatessen and buy a brick of ice cream. This would only happen once every two or three weeks. The brick was small and flat, designed to fit into the very small freezer compartment of refrigerators of the time. The vanilla-flavoured, white ice cream was wrapped in cardboard with attractive writing on the outside - AMSCOL ICE CREAM. It was an oblong shape, much like a building brick. We enthusiastically consumed it shortly after it was bought.

With the availability of ice cream now, birthday parties are the best excuse to scoop out the luxurious creamy white food.

People in the Bible put a big emphasis on their celebrations. Jesus may not have eaten ice cream, but he grew up understanding the meaning of feasts, banquets and special food. A very significant time was the Last Supper, where Jesus ate the Passover meal with his disciples. It was his last meal with them. Some important conversations took place at that meal. Jesus spelled out clearly that he was facing the end of his earthly life and someone in their presence would betray him, leaving the rest to disperse.

The Last Supper should have been an extremely sad party because the guest of honour was saying his final goodbye, but the disciples did not fully understand what would happen to their beloved Jesus. For generations, they had been accustomed to the Passover meal being celebrated. Jesus promised his disciples that he would go ahead of them after he had risen. We need to know that for ourselves, too.

"Lord God, we appreciate how you keep the future hidden from us. Please help us not to take ice cream and celebrations for granted. Thank you, Jesus."

Matthew 26: 29-32
"I tell you, I will not drink of this fruit of the vine from now on until that day when I drink it anew with you in my Father's Kingdom". When they had sung a hymn, they went out to the Mount of Olives. Then Jesus told them, "This very night you will all fall away on account of me, for it is written: 'I will strike the shepherd, and the sheep of the flock will be scattered.' But after I have risen, I will go ahead of you into Galilee."

'Just a Reminder-Each Day'

February 19

Optimistic or Pessimistic

The radio announcer suggested that the piece of music he was about to play would be like waking up and seeing the sunshine; being excited about what the day may bring. I was not sure that the music did it for me, but it did get me thinking about optimism. Children are more likely to be optimistic than adults. There were years when we visited our daughter and family and used their caravan as our accommodation. Each day started with an interesting noise. The family lived in a transportable house with wooden floors. Their children, ranging in age from preschool to late primary school, were allowed to go to the lounge room and watch television if they woke early. This allowed the parents a little more sleep. From the time they could run, the children ran from their bedrooms to the lounge room on the wooden floorboards. The sound of their footsteps echoed out to where we were sleeping. That was fine. At least we knew when someone was up. Gradually they have outgrown that childlike excitement at the beginning of the day and now the older ones are just like the rest of us as they slowly make their way to the kitchen with sleep in their eyes and hair everywhere.

Feeling optimistic about life rather than pessimistic is a great way to start the day. Some people have trouble getting a good start while others don't. Seeing life through God's eyes gives us a more confident start. Healthy morning rituals like Bible reading and prayer may just help us to be optimistic about the day.

It is a huge privilege to have someone pray for us each day. If you don't have this support, maybe you and a friend can agree to pray for each other. God is not limited by distance. 'Find a friend and pray!'

"Lord God, I give myself to you, body, mind, soul and spirit, that you may have your way in my life today. Equip, encourage and show me what you and I together can do. Thank you, Jesus."

Psalm 92: 1
It is good to praise the Lord and make music to your name, O Most High, to proclaim your love in the morning and your faithfulness at night.

'Just a Reminder-Each Day'

Mistaken Identity

The black cat was looking intently, but I could not see anything moving in the garden. Then she looked away. Mistaken identity, I presumed. How often do we hear people say, "I swear I saw you coming out of the shop until the person turned their head?" It is easy enough to mistake a person from a distance.

When I see statues of Buddhas in people's homes, shops or gardens, I wonder if it is just a case of mistaken identity. The statue is supposed to bring peace – a nice idea, but can it? It appears that people are genuine when they choose to have a Buddha in their place. They want real peace and tranquillity. Statues that are supposed to bring peace, symbols that charm and idols that are worshipped are common enough in our society. Some religions light candles to gods to ward off sickness or keep bad spirits away.

There is a hidden danger when we think a statue or other god can give us what we need. The Biblical Living God says there will be no other god than him, and we should worship him only. He alone has the power and authority to do what we mistakenly think an idol or statue can.

It was Jesus who offered people his peace during his time on earth. Even when he was going back to heaven, he promised to leave his peace. This promise of peace is from a living identity, one who can be with us always. There is no mistaken identity in Jesus.

"Lord God, please help me to see if I am relying on something which contradicts my faith in you. Thank you, Jesus."

Exodus 20: 1-4
I am the Lord your God who brought you out of Egypt, out of the land of slavery. You shall have no other gods before me. You shall not make for yourselves an idol in the form of anything in heaven above or on earth beneath or in the waters below.

Can't Find God

A very elusive document has my husband and me feeling rather frustrated. We have looked everywhere for it, discussed where it could be, hunted high and low and, in desperation, we have prayed together but still have not found it. I guess there are times in everyone's life when they have been unable to find something. However, if we can't find God we feel frustrated, abandoned, or even angry.

King David said he felt like a worm, not a man when he could not find God (Psalm 22:1-11). Job lost his farm and family and wondered where God was, but he declared God was not against him (Job 23: 1-9). The rich young man who approached Jesus to see what he had to do to inherit eternal life had actually found God, but unable to accept the conditions of giving up his wealth, he turned his back on Jesus and went away. He could not give up the very thing that defined him (Mark 10:17-21). Jesus, hanging on the cross, uttered the saddest words of all; "My God, why have you forsaken me?" (Mark 15:34). They all experienced the feeling of separation from God.

It can be hard to find God when we feel sick, lonely, afraid or depressed. Personal troubles, work, distracted by the bright lights and worldly concerns can isolate us from God, too.

On the other side of death, the risen Jesus tells his disciples that he will be with them always, even to the end of time (Matt. 29: 20).

If only we could see that God is with us all the time. This can be tough, but with the Spirit's help, we can trust that his presence never leaves us.

True, we can't find God sometimes – but he sees us all the time!

"Lord God, in our dark times of being unable to find you or feel your love and support, please come to us and rescue us. Thank you, Jesus."

Hosea 6: 3
Let us acknowledge the Lord; let us press on to acknowledge him. As surely as the sun rises, he will appear; he will come to us like winter rains, like the spring rains that water the earth.

February 22
Hens and Chicks

A hen walking along with her brood of chicks can be pretty entertaining. She talks to them and if danger presents itself, she squats and fluffs her feathers out, creating a shelter and the chicks scurry under her. Sometimes in less urgent situations a couple of chickens will jump onto their mother's back and hide in the feathers or snuggle down with only their heads peeping up.

A hen without chickens can make a nice pet. Our granddaughters carry their hens around, occasionally giving one a ride on the bike with them. When a hen is sitting on eggs or with new chickens, she can be quite protective, snappy, and willing to peck any hand that gets too near her nest. An aggressive hen will leave her nest and chase away any intruders. The hen can be passive one minute and aggressive the next; each mood and action serves a purpose.

Jesus said he wished he could have gathered the people of Jerusalem up like a hen gathers her chickens. We read that Jesus was putting himself in the same position as many of the prophets before him. They all had this in common; they were God's messengers to bring people back to God. In this Bible reading, Jesus had just mentioned his death, warning his followers that his fate was the same as the prophets who had already lost their lives.

Jesus is not an ordinary human being offering to take care of a nation. He is God calling his people to run to him, trust him and shelter under his wings. A hen can only take care of her chickens, but God offers all humanity his care. God has given Jesus all authority against the enemy of this world. Jesus is our protector.

Running to Jesus does more than shelter us, it sets us up for a life of support and empowerment. It continues to be an offer too good to turn down.

"Lord God, help us to hear you calling, offering us your protection. We have everything to gain from trusting you and nothing to lose. Thank you, Jesus."

Luke 13:34
O Jerusalem, Jerusalem, you who kill the prophets and stone those sent to you, how often I have longed to gather your children together as a hen gathers her chicks under her wings, but you were not willing!

'Just a Reminder-Each Day'

Don't Trip or You May Fall

The one big concept that trips so many people up, is Jesus the man who claimed to be God. The Jewish people believed certain things about God like he was an out-of-this-world being that no one could even look at. They believed that he was seated on a throne in heaven beyond reaching and if you did see him, you would die. When Moses was in the presence of God on the mountain, he glowed so brightly that people could not look at him. This was how it was for people in the Old Testament times. They believed God was the power behind the thunder, lightning, fire and earthquakes.

In New Testament times, people happily followed Jesus around and were captivated by his miracles but some didn't necessarily acknowledge him as the Messiah or Son of God. The apostle Paul, called Saul, hunted down people who were followers of Jesus. He was convinced they were way off the track! But many did believe Jesus was the Son of God and it is their testimony that has helped to shape Christianity, change the world and even shape our lives.

People today still get tripped up admiring the works of Jesus but are unable to accept him as God. We have the massive advantage of knowing the end of the story. Jesus, the man, died and rose from the dead. He then appeared to thousands, disappeared through crowds and turned up through closed doors, all the while proving his victory over death. This man was no ordinary man! As hard as it seems, to be saved, we must believe that Jesus is one with God and is God. The hard-to-believe truth can trip us up but, if we just give Jesus a go, we will be richly rewarded.

"Lord God, I admire the man Jesus; please help me to see him as God and Saviour, my saviour. Thank you, Jesus."

John 5:46
(Jesus speaking) If you believed Moses, you would believe me because he wrote about me.

John 6: 68
(Simon Peter replies to Jesus) Lord, to whom shall we go? You have the words of eternal life. We believe and know that you are the Holy One of God.

'Just a Reminder-Each Day'

More to Show Us

My daughter learnt over to smell the roses. This was one of those special moments where she was taking time to enjoy the same things that I do. As we wandered around the garden, we looked to find which plants were giving off a strong perfume. I don't have the privilege of talking about gardens with my daughter very often. We live many hours apart and visits are usually busy family times. There is much pleasure in showing someone around our homes and gardens. Visitors to our farm were usually given the grand tour via the 4WD through the property to see crops, sheep and pastures. To complete the tour, we would stop at the machinery shed and invite our guests to climb up into the big equipment. On some occasions, my husband has given young city ladies a drive of a tractor or header, very slowly around the big yard. Some girls take to it excitedly, while others giggle with embarrassment or fear! Another place of interest is the stables where animal lovers can pat the horses.

When we visit family interstate, we are often taken to the rain forest and lookout at Coffs Harbour where we marvel at the tall trees and rough sea in the distance. When our Japanese friend visited us, she was amazed at the vastness of our country. Showing her the Australian landscape gave pleasure to both her and us.

In God's creation, there is always something amazing to see. God wants to show us more than just the things that grow, move and delight us. He wants us to see and experience Him as Father, His Son as our Saviour and the Holy Spirit as His life in us.

"Lord God, I thank you for the wonderful privilege of getting to know you. Thank you that we can experience things with your Spirit that were once hidden from us. Thank you, Jesus."

1 Chronicles 29: 11
Yours, O Lord, is the greatness, power, glory, majesty, and splendour, for everything in heaven and earth is yours. Yours, O Lord is the kingdom; you are exalted as head over all.

Memorabilia – Remember Jesus

Do you love to keep things, save memorabilia, attend reunions, collect souvenirs on holidays, pin photos up and reminisce with old friends, or maybe you don't need to remember as much as other people do? In the television program, 'The Farmer Wants a Wife,' one farmer admitted to wearing his late father's boots in memory of him. Some people lose valuable family history through theft, fire, floods, storms or having to move to a smaller home. Remembering does play an important part in our lives. Jesus said, 'Do this in remembrance of me.' A church should be a good place where we are reminded of what Jesus has done for us and continues to do through his Holy Spirit. Some people say they are Christians but don't need to attend church. If a church activity reminds us of God's goodness, it may benefit us if we add it to our diary. For some people, church attendance doesn't work.

When I think I can live without any community worship, I am reminded of the benefits there are in sharing my faith and experiences with others. I believe memorabilia plays a big part in our well-being.

The years of learning about God have built me up, mended a few broken parts and given me a different perspective on life. Jesus is worth celebrating, and there is always more to discover. A church should benefit us, but sometimes it is hard to find that place where we feel we belong. It may be that we need to contribute to the church of our choice and add value to it through our faithful attendance. There is nothing wrong but plenty right in praying for a church to meet our individual needs.

"Lord God, remind us of the role you have already played in our lives. Please help us to enjoy and celebrate your goodness. If you want us to take part in some Christian group or church, please give us the lead we need. Thank you, Jesus."

Acts 2: 42,43
They devoted themselves to the apostles' teaching and to the fellow-ship, to the breaking of bread and to prayer. Everyone was filled with awe, and the apostles did many wonders and miraculous signs.

'Just a Reminder-Each Day'

Have We Lost Our Connection?

Early Australian homes were single-storey, square houses with a veranda that ran all the way around. People would sit or stand on any side of the house under their verandas, in the shade or out of the rain and look out over their land or down their street. This was a common way of connecting with the outdoors, visitors, people passing by and what was happening in their district and neighbourhood.

Modern homes look more like no one is home until you go through the front door. Sometimes they are two-storey and rarely with a veranda. If you are lucky to have the space, the backyard becomes the private entertainment place with an undercover eating area and a pool close by. The connection with community, neighbours, or friends passing by seems less present here. It is exclusive rather than inclusive.

So many jobs today are alone indoors, even the man on the land sits in a tractor cabin with a screen that tells him if anything needs attention. So, he doesn't have to get out or relate personally to anyone for hours. Our lives can be tied to a stringent routine with little flexibility. No time to casually connect with people or our environment. We build up businesses, using less staff, only to eventually replace these workers with technical shortcuts.

Have we lost the ability to connect to our environment, the people around us and more importantly the One who gave us all of this? In the following Bible story, a disabled person is doing his best to get connected to someone who will help him and to God's healing power.

"Lord God, please reset our way of life if we have moved too far from the best lifestyle for us. Help us breathe the air, watch the sunset, reconnect with you, and know what really matters in life. Thank you, Jesus."

John 5: 1-9
Here a great number of disabled people used to lie – the blind, the lame, the paralysed. One who was there had been an invalid for thirty-eight years. When Jesus saw him lying there and learned that he had been in that condition for a long time, he asked him, "Do you want to get well?" "Sir," the invalid replied, "I have no-one to help me into the pool when the water is stirred." Then Jesus said to him, "Get up. Pick up your mat and walk." At once the man was cured.

'Just a Reminder-Each Day'

Conflict
(Why do we have to have it?)

I took the dog walking to pick up some rubbish from our bin that went flying down the street in a big wind. It was a very short walk. When we turned to come home, I knew the dog was disappointed. This was not her usual walk to the beach. Back home I patted her and apologised. She put her head in my lap and accepted a pat as compensation. I couldn't help thinking what a difference there is between having a pet who accepts what they cannot understand and a child who does not want to accept what they can understand.

That is why pets make such good companions. To have a child who can ask questions and interact with us on a much deeper level than a pet is even more rewarding. It is a miracle how a child's brain develops and navigates its way through life, gaining understanding and wisdom as it goes.

All too soon our children have grown up. The business of driving them to school, sports and hobbies, keeping up with clothes, food, extra education and financial support, loses its intensity. Adulthood can present a different set of problems. We can complain about the tensions we are experiencing with our adult children or find a solution.

One day, as my friend and I walked back to our cars, I felt led to ask her about family matters and she took the opportunity to give me an update. We talked about conflict, personality clashes and differences of opinion between two generations trying to work together. We agreed that finding God's solution to some hurtful problems was a good place to start.

"Lord God, you are the creator of families, friendships and groups where all too often we run into trouble. Please give us your solution. Help us to find answers to complex relational problems. Please give us the grace to forgive, the willingness to apologise and the ability to make things right. Help us to see each other through your eyes, to love each other and accept our differences. Thank you, Jesus."

1Corinthians 1: 10
I appeal to you brothers, in the name of our Lord Jesus Christ, that all of you agree with one another so that there be no divisions among you and that you may be perfectly united in mind and thought.

'Just a Reminder-Each Day'

February 28

Spiritual Experience

The music composer John Williams can be accredited for taking us, the viewers of dramatic films like Jaws, E.T., Indiana Jones, Jurassic Park and Superman, into the real spirit of the film. It is amazing how effective music is in films to carry the audience along in a very convincing way. We experience terror, relief, excitement, victory, love and a range of other emotions, all because of the music in the background.

Music plays an integral part in the church, youth events and many other places of worship. Over the years, we have been involved in camps, where the style of music has changed. The purpose and intent have remained sincere in its desire to bring people closer to God. Lyrics and melodies can lift our spirits, help us to connect to God's Spirit and discover another dimension to our faith.

We are spiritual beings, so our spirit needs to find happiness and fulfilment too. We are designed to worship the One who created us and to go to Him and enjoy our spiritual connection. Too much mood music, clapping, dancing and getting carried away spiritually have given some Pentecostal Churches and youth events a bad name. God calls us to worship him with music and joy, so we need to see if there is a good outcome before condemning something we are unsure of.

"Lord God, please help us come into your presence with music in our hearts and enjoy the connection with you. Thank you, Jesus."

Sing joyfully to the Lord you righteous; it is fitting for the upright to praise him. Praise the Lord with the harp; make music to him on the ten-stringed lyre. Sing to him a new song; play skilfully, and shout for joy.

Unfair Expectations

Ash Barty was asked after winning Wimbledon in 2021 what she was thinking during the last point. She said, "I don't remember". The media are in the habit of expecting athletes in any sport to be eloquent, inspired speakers. Swimmers straight out of the pool, tennis players straight off the court, jockeys still cantering back to the weighing-in yard and runners straight off the track are all expected to have something amazing to say even though their chests are heaving, sweat is dripping down their faces and their minds are winding down from the strain of trying to win.

Who expects this? Do the media alone expect it, or do we the viewers expect it, too? Isn't this an unfair expectation? God doesn't have unfair expectations of us. We do tend to put that on ourselves and others. The apostle Paul suggests that people can have special abilities (gifts), but he doesn't indicate they are meant to have them all. Just like an athlete should not be expected to be an eloquent speaker, so we ought to be able to use the gifts we are given, but not be under pressure to also have other gifts.

"Lord God, thank you for the gifts you have given us; please help us to use them wisely. Lord, help us recognise the gifts you have given others and not expect too much of them. Thank you, Jesus."

1 Corinthians 7: 7
But each man has his own gift from God; one has this gift, another has that.

March 1
Day Perfect

Show me a perfect day!

Trying to describe a perfect temperature, I thought it was probably skin temperature, neither hot nor cold, just perfect. The air was perfectly still, not a bird flying or a moth landing and the plants looked greener than green because a soaking summer rain had fallen the week before. New shoots adorned the tops of shrubs and the leaves on the trees shone with happiness. Soft white clouds decorated a perfect pastel blue sky. Everything looked and smelt perfect.

Out of the stillness of the day, the annoying muffled buzz of a March fly caught our attention. It flew overhead, invisible until it landed. Then the dog got annoyed, snapping her jaws with huge determination to put an end to the intruder. I don't know how many March flies turned up in the garden because they have a way of being heard and not seen until they land on you. Before you can get your brain into gear to make a swipe at it, it is gone! Even the cat, causally sprawled out enjoying the perfect day, had to have a swipe at it, not just once or twice but three or four swipes for good measure.

Life is like that. Just when you think you've got the perfect moment on a perfect day, it is spoilt. But if we have the God-given ability to see how perfect the day is without letting the enemy spoil it, we are better off.

"Lord God, there is no doubt this world is far from perfect but thank you for those special times when it seems almost there. Thank you, Jesus."

Job 2: 7-10
So, Satan went out from the presence of the Lord and afflicted Job with painful sores from the soles of his feet to the top of his head. Then Job took a piece of broken pottery and scraped himself with it as he sat among the ashes. His wife said to him, "Are you still holding onto your integrity? Curse God and die!"

He replied, "You are talking like a foolish woman. Shall we accept good from God and not trouble?" In all this, Job did not sin in what he said.

‘Just a Reminder-Each Day’

Complaints

Complaints can be a big stumbling block in running events. They can cause us to stagger or even fall before we realise what is going wrong. If we step up to organise an event, it is quite possible we will run into some conflict. An email from an unhappy parent sat unread in my inbox until I felt equipped to manage the complaint. Over the years of running youth camps, I have learned that I need some recovery time before managing difficult issues. I cannot be kind or gracious when I am exhausted. I certainly can't manage problems wisely when my emotions are getting in the way. With my head in my hands, I waited on the Lord, asking him for help. I continued waiting. Gradually I could see the problem from the unhappy parent's perspective. Instead of feeling accused, with God's help, I was able to talk to her about the problem as if I were another parent experiencing the same injustice. These encounters hurt initially but as God steps in and his Holy Spirit comforts both parties, a sense of peace prevails.

The Holy Spirit enables the person with the complaint to feel heard. The accused person can feel the loving support of the Father and his protection, even after bowing down to the accuser and apologising. Like a doormat but not trodden on.

When Jesus went to the cross, an innocent man, he was spat on, accused wrongly, given a crown of thorns to wear, insulted and taunted but through all that he trusted his Heavenly Father for victory.

Paul, the writer of Philippians, knew what it was like to suffer. In his striving to bring people back to God the Father, he went through many hardships. Our testimony, based on our experience of knowing Jesus, is highly valuable in leading people back to God.

"Lord God, please teach me to manage complaints and dissatisfaction with grace and genuine care for the other person. Thank you, Jesus."

Philippians 2: 4
Do everything without complaining or arguing so that you may become blameless and pure, children of God without fault in a crooked and depraved generation, in which you shine like stars in the universe as you hold out to the word of life – in order that I may boast on the day of Christ that I did not run or labour for nothing.

Discerning

During an Easter Camp, just after one of the teaching sessions had finished, a leader came to me and asked if I would come and help pray for a camper. Occasionally I would be asked to help where discerning something was proving difficult. Just for the record, there were times when I was completely unable to discern the person's problem. Most often, the problem proved to be something the young person had been dabbling in like, reading star signs for guidance, having an imaginary friend or just opposing the authority of God. Walking down the long passageway, my mind was already thinking through what this person's problem might be. I was envisioning some of the typical traps young people fall into. This camper was new to us, so I was about to pray for someone I knew absolutely nothing about. Before I started asking him about what he may have been involved in, that would have hindered his relationship with God, I hesitated. Then I asked the Lord again for discernment. I was shown that this young man was on a sincere journey of faith in Jesus and the stumbling block was not of his making but it was a specific evil obstruction. The leader and I took charge of the presence of evil in Jesus' Name, casting it out. We saw the young man freed. It was a simple easy prayer with an incredible feeling of victory for all of us.

When I walked away, I could not help thanking God that I had not accused that young man of doing something he had not done. Later in the year, he and some friends came to stay on our farm. It was a fun weekend for all of us.

"Lord God, I thank you for trusting me with some of your spiritual gifts. Please give me courage as I venture into unknown territory and help me to be aware that you are in charge, not me. Thank you, Jesus."

1 Corinthians 12: 7-10
Now to each one the manifestation of the Spirit is given for the common good. To one there is given through the Spirit the message of wisdom, to another the message of knowledge by means of the same Spirit, to another faith by the same Spirit, to another gifts of healing by that one Spirit, to another miraculous powers, to another prophecy, to another distinguishing between spirits, to another speaking in different kinds of tongues, and to still another the interpretation of tongues.

'Just a Reminder-Each Day'

Beautiful People

We should be exceptionally grateful to be living in our part of the Western world. Very few of us struggle to have our daily needs met. Most of us have enough food, clothes, shelter and a regular income, which allows us to think of other things like acquiring some luxuries.

Beach holidays are popular, like a simple tent on the beach or elaborate accommodation with a sea view. Beaches are places where beautiful people can Obe on display! Women with beautiful bodies, long flowing hair and engaging eyes catch our attention. Men showing off their muscular, tanned frames are not hard to find either. Beauty is an interesting term. By what standards do we evaluate beauty? The Bible mentions beautiful people like Job's daughters, Queen Esther and the virgin brought in to comfort King David who was an athletic, appealing man in his youth.

It would be unfair if those people who are beautiful on the outside were the happiest, but that is not necessarily the case. It seems that those who have inner peace, hope, satisfaction, faith and purpose, regardless of their outward appearance, might even be happier.

In one of our earlier youth camps, our song leader started one session by encouraging the girls to dress up a little. "Come on girls," she said, "I know it's OK to dress a bit daggy on camps, but we can also put a bit of effort in and make ourselves look nice". She led by example wearing nice colourful clothes and accessories. Most girls continued to wear their comfy' camp clothes.

In Christian circles, there will always be differences of opinion about an acceptable dress code for women, but too much controversy detracts from the real meaning of Christianity.

"Lord God, we ask for your wisdom in presenting ourselves. Please help us to be appreciative of our looks and free from envy and low self-esteem. Please help us recognise the inner beauty you give each of us. Thank you, Jesus."

1 Peter 3: 3,4
Your beauty should not come from outward adornments, such as braided hair and wearing gold jewellery and fine clothes. Instead, it should be that of your inner self, the unfading beauty of a gentle and quiet spirit, which is of great worth in God's sight.

Out of Tragedy

I met my husband about 14 years after his family had been through the tragedy of losing a three-year-old child in a farming accident. I learnt to greatly admire my in-laws, especially coming to understand how they managed that life-changing event. In the very first year of our marriage, a revival was sweeping across our nation in various districts. International evangelists were brought to the capital cities to share their faith. Many other smaller events took place in churches and halls where gifted speakers and ordinary people shared their stories of what God was doing. Those events drew big crowds. My in-laws were occasional church-going people but this revival enabled them to get to know Jesus with more assurance. It was common at those revival rallies for people to be called forward to receive prayer. My father-in-law often went forward. At one rally, while receiving prayer, he said he felt God say to him, "My child, my precious child." Each time he told people about his experience, his eyes lit up. Those who knew Dad's heartache understood why he needed to hear those words from his Lord.

After the death of their three-year-old daughter, my in-laws could have become angry with God, shut themselves off from society or become hardened people. Still, as they became empowered by God's Spirit during the revival, they gained new direction for their lives. They enthusiastically attended as many rallies as possible, always taking their children and anyone else's children who could fit in their car.

Their home became a drop-in place for people of all ages, but predominately young people. They continued to support every Christian event in their area, particularly youth events. My Father-in-law loved nurturing young people, teaching them Christian songs and sharing his God experiences with anyone who wanted to hear. He had positioned himself and his family to receive as much of God as possible. This has resulted in what could have been a wasted life becoming a family that has been a big influence, particularly in the lives of people seeking Jesus.

Lord God, we thank you for families who are significantly influential in leading people to you. Thank you, Jesus."

1 John 4: 13
We know that we live in him and he is us, because he has given us of his Spirit.

Running on Empty

The trouble with running on empty is that we have nothing left to draw from, let alone being able to help others. It can happen to all of us at any stage. We can find ourselves being grumpy, impatient, irritable and expecting too much of others. Running on empty means our energy has already been sapped. It blocks out the positives in our lives and robs us of happiness. Getting out of bed can be hard; trying to think clearly and being organised is not fun either. We may blame ourselves or others for the state we are in; "If I got a bit more support, I wouldn't be so tired", "It's not fair that I get left with everything!"

These feelings are hard to manage. James 5:16 advises us to admit our faults to one another and pray for each other so that we may be healed. Rather than blame ourselves or others, it works better to admit our needs and emptiness to someone we can trust and ask for their prayers. If our fuel tank has run very low, it is less likely that we will be miraculously refilled all at once. Although God could do that, more likely, a regular pattern of rest, prayer and support is best for a recovery that will last. Lean on Him daily.

I have found in my recovery time that God is teaching me ways of avoiding a breakdown in the future. I don't like admitting I can't do something, but in my weakness, God leads me to appreciate and accept the skills of others. If I can let him have his way, I realise he is guiding me to live a more stable life.

Psychologist professor John Parker, on addressing the loss of energy and emotional breakdowns, said the people prone to break down are usually good people trying to do good!

Regaining our strength and confidence often looks out of reach but taking one day at a time and positioning ourselves for good support is a very positive way to recover.

"Lord God, when I am empty, please show me how to get filled up. Please protect me from getting too low before I ask for help. I put my mental and physical needs in your hands. Thank you, Jesus."

Psalm 42: 5,6
Why are you downcast O my soul? Why so disturbed within me? Put your hope in God, for I will yet praise him, my Saviour and my God.

March 7
Whoops!

It had been fun riding our horses along the quiet, country back roads and into a scrub paddock. Pony Club picnics were a time of adventure and exploration for our small group of twelve children and three adults. We didn't see a car or any other vehicle for the long one-hour ride. Later, some parents brought food in their cars and met us in a small clearing in the scrub, where we each tied our horses to a tree while we enjoyed our lunch. As young riders, we had formed close friendships since our Pony Club started.

Finally, it was time to saddle up again. There was more fun to be had riding through the scrub and finding logs to jump. I'm surprised I didn't realise what was about to happen to me, but I fell for it! Everyone was getting their horse ready for remounting. I thought I was prepared. I gathered my reins on Velvet, my pony so that she wouldn't walk forward, then I put my left foot in the stirrup to mount up, but just as I did, the saddle slipped towards me! I scrambled and hopped and fell to the ground! Getting back onto my feet and wondering what had just happened, I realised I was surrounded by a group of cheeky boys, almost rolling on the ground laughing. I had been set up! They had loosened my girth straps on the opposite side when I wasn't looking. Then it all came back to me. One of the boys had distracted me while another one must have loosened the girth. I think I enjoyed the attention, especially when I realised what a fun trick it was.

Being in a group of trusted friends where we can play tricks on each other and have a laugh is a good environment to be in. It is hard to find where Jesus engaged in any humorous events. He was on a very serious mission, but there must have been times when he and his close friends laughed together.

There have been occasions in my life where I have been convinced that God did something specific, which caused me to laugh. God is the author of all our emotions, so let's enjoy laughing.

"Lord God, we thank you for our good relationships where we can laugh and trust each other completely. Thank you, Jesus."

Psalm 126: 2
Our mouths were filled with laughter, our tongues with songs of joy, then it was said among the nations, "The Lord has done great things for them."

March 8

Surprise Me

I t can be fun to surprise someone. Parents often try and surprise their children with presents, parties and visitors. Not all surprises are good. A friend of ours attended the Royal Show in Adelaide and returned to the car park at the end of the evening, for the two-hour drive to get home, only to find his car had been stolen! A very unhappy surprise.

I have found God to be into surprises. I don't know if he does it for fun, but they are always nice surprises. We have been looking to buy a house, but no matter how hard I look, I haven't found one that suits us. I am often surprised when we arrive home from a weekend away to see a For Sale sign on a house that may suit us. So far, it hasn't worked out, but it is always a pleasant surprise to find that God may have something for us one day. Frequently when I ask God for specific directions on a matter where an answer isn't needed immediately, it comes when I least expect it. I'm not sure why it works that way, but I believe God uses surprises.

In this Bible reading, the greatest surprise of all time will be the return of Jesus. But note here that even though it sounds like bad news for some, the writer is reassuring the followers of Jesus that this big surprise will not catch them out!

"Lord God, thank you for the promise of preparing us for your return. Thank you, Jesus."

Now, brothers, about times and dates we do not need to write to you, for you know very well that the day of the Lord will come like a thief in the night. While people are saying, "Peace and safety" destruction will come on them suddenly, as labour pains on a pregnant woman, and they will not escape. But you, brothers, are not in darkness so that this day should surprise you like a thief. You are all sons of the light and sons of the day. We do not belong to the night or to the darkness.

Across Cultures

It is a long time ago that I was in primary school, but I have a vivid memory of a new girl in school. She stood out with her extremely short hairstyle, one which we conservative country girls thought should only be seen on a boy. She also had a ring in her ear. I am not sure if anyone we knew had pierced ears; we certainly had not seen that before. The poor girl had to explain that in England, where she came from, short hair and pierced ears were very fashionable. As the years went by, television proved her right. We got over the shock.

Decades later we invited an Aboriginal Islander man to speak at our youth camp. We soon learnt that some people hug more freely than we do, laugh more enthusiastically and are more openly affectionate than us. We had a wonderful camp with Rodney as he shared his love of God and encouraged us to be more expectant of God. We also learnt to brace ourselves ready for his huge hugs which nearly broke our ribs. It happened often.

God also taught us that people of other cultures are no different from us. Our God is the God of all creation, all cultures and all who are yet to believe in Jesus as their Saviour. Acts 10 says that God anointed Jesus of Nazareth with the Holy Spirit and power; he went around doing good, freeing everyone under the influence of the devil because God was with him.

"Lord God, please help us accept people from other cultures and see them as you see them. Thank you, Jesus."

Acts 10: 28, 34
God has shown me that I should not call any man impure or unclean.
Then Peter began to speak; "I now realise how true it is that God does not show favouritism but accepts men from every nation who fear him and do what is right."

March 10

Names

Names play an essential part in our culture. We encourage our babies to recognise their names as young as possible. Most people spend time choosing names for their children and then some people unknowingly set their children up with names that invite ridicule. Some people have chosen to change their names, while other names have become famous. Many names have been lost in the crowd of familiarity. In the book, 'Johnny Cash-The Redemption of an American Icon' Johnny was given a song written by Shel Silverstein to record. The song was called, 'A Boy Named Sue', which told the story of *a ne'er-do-well father who gave his son a girl's name to make him grow up quick and grow up mean, and never step aside for anyone.* The song did extremely well in the music charts and later won Johnny a Grammy for the best Male Country Vocal Performance.

I did not have any church upbringing, so I had a lot to learn when I became a Christian. One concept that intrigued my friends and me was the 'Name of Jesus.' We were experiencing God in a new way. We read books on the topic, discussed all the possibilities and listened to teaching wherever we could. Books about the Name of Jesus helped me to believe in its power and where it could be applied to everyday life.

I gradually gained confidence that Jesus wasn't joking when he said we could use his name and expect to see results. Speaking in his name to oppose the forces of evil and to take control of a situation was revolutionary to me. It was power to be used for our good and the good of others.

As I learned to put this concept into practice, I found being a Christian had turned into an exciting adventure.

"Lord God, thank you for allowing us to use your name against our enemies and to break down volatile situations. Thank you, Jesus."

Philippians 2: 9,10
Therefore God exalted him to the highest place and gave him the name that is above every name, that at the name of Jesus every knee should bow in heaven and on earth and under the earth.

March 11
Tenting

Camping can be so much fun but erecting tents can be less fun. At least it was decades ago when tents were difficult, time-consuming and frustrating to erect. I am glad our dads came to the rescue at Pony Club camps and set up our tents. I have good memories of happy chatting girlfriends, in our tents, laying on our camp stretchers, talking until we fell asleep. Years later, as instructors, we had fun checking tents for tidiness. One group of very inventive campers found a way of making their tent look better than the rest. They hid the only broom available in one of their beds!

Later in my life, during a very wet Easter when our Christian camp was held near a creek, the experience was quite different. The rain kept falling all night and by morning we were seeing young people appearing from their tents, wet. They had wet bedding and some wet clothes, too. That caused us a great deal of work finding ways to get everything dry.

Anyone who has camped in a tent will have a tent story to tell. At a Kid's Camp Out weekend, the wind blew hard. Many adults were outside the tents late at night, in their pyjamas, re-pegging, and pulling ropes tighter while trying not to trip over them or wake the young occupants.

Tents are a vulnerable form of housing. The Israelites knew all about tenting. The Old Testament refers to tents often. This Bible reading talks about making God our dwelling place because our lives are like tents, in need of protection.

"Lord God, thank you for the protection you offer us, whether in our tent or out. Thank you, Jesus."

Psalm 91: 9, 10
If you make the Most High your dwelling- even the Lord, who is my refuge-then no harm will befall you, no disaster will come near your tent.

‘Just a Reminder-Each Day’

I have No Idea

We have experienced many very enjoyable moments over the years at the youth camps we have been involved with. One such moment was a sharing time when campers told us what was happening for them at camp. Eliza, a warm and friendly older teen, entertained us with her story, but after a while, she paused and said, "I have no idea where this is going!" We all laughed a little, but almost immediately, she remembered and went on to tell us of her encounter with God and what it meant to her. It was a moment that stuck with me because the setting was perfect. In the picturesque chapel at Melrose, the large windows allow you to gaze in wonder at the scene outside. The forest of tall eucalyptus trees leads up to Mount Remarkable, which seems to reach for the sky. This uniquely beautiful sight was a part of Eliza's story, as she had grown up close to that place.

From time to time, during the writing of this book, I have found myself saying, "I have no idea where this is going!" Then I am reminded (probably by God) that this was his idea and it is not up to me to work out where the story is going, just to wait on him and write what he tells me, even if it is the next day.

We all have these moments, even years when we have no idea where we are going but God, who has a good plan for us and wants the best for us, encourages us to be strong and wait on him.

"Lord God, for those of us who have no idea where we are going, we ask for your direction and leading. If we do already know, we ask for your continuing guidance. Thank you, Jesus."

Psalm 27: 13,14
I am still confident of this: I will see the goodness of the Lord in the land of the living. Wait for the Lord; be strong and take heart and wait for the Lord.

Each Stage in Life

It was the end of another enjoyable but tiring youth camp. Leaders went about packing the sporting, stage and sound equipment while others cleaned rooms and packed tables and chairs away. Some younger campers had already been collected by their parents for the trip home, while others lingered, not wanting to leave. A few wandered around in the lazy sun or just sat and talked. A teenage girl who had just spent her third camp with us went over to a teenage guy and gave him a friendly lingering hug. The two had been getting to know each other over a few years of attending the same camps. They kept in touch on a casual basis between camps.

During the years of running these camps, we have dealt with some undesirable teenage behaviour. Some young people, who seem to have no idea about relating to the opposite sex, have caused us concern. Sadly, they would not be doing themselves any favours by secretly going off at night, experimenting with relationships and getting involved too quickly. These are some ways teenagers mess up their lives.

I went about packing up, feeling very relieved that the two campers who chose to hug each other to say goodbye did it openly and with respect for each other. It is this kind of relationship that encourages me to help young people connect with God as young as possible.

This was a good sign of the Holy Spirit giving wisdom to these young people, helping them through the awkward stages. Without God's guidance, they may have let their feelings rule their behaviour.

I believe parents should pursue a close relationship with God and pray that their children/teenagers will find it too. It is usually rewarding.

"Lord God, thank you for training young people, by your Spirit living in them, to trust you and live a life of wisdom and integrity. Thank you, Jesus."

Romans 8: 9
You, however, are controlled not by the sinful nature but by the Spirit, if the Spirit of God lives in you.

March 14

In a Secret Place

f I had not been waiting for my desktop computer to warm up, I would have missed what was happening in a secret place. My eyes were drawn to the heart of my large rose bush in its leafiest part. A New Holland Honey Eater bird flew into a nest. Once in the bush, I could not see it at all! But the bird had managed to leave some evidence. A strip of white wool was left dangling out of the nest, the only clue that anything was happening in that secret place.

From the window of my home office, I often catch a glimpse of the birds flying in and out of the nest.

We, humans, miss a lot of what happens in secret places. It takes time and patience to sit and observe nature at work. We know the reason why small birds build their nests in secluded places, but why did Jesus suggest we go into our rooms and shut the door to pray? I guess there have always been distractions while praying, even in Jesus' time. It's almost unbelievable that our Heavenly Father desires some one-to-one time with us alone in a secret place. Accepting that he does, who knows what revelation we may have in that very personal time with him.

"Lord God, help us to make time to meet with you and to understand the importance of not being distracted. Please draw us aside each day to teach us your ways and build us up. Thank you, Jesus."

'Just a Reminder-Each Day'

Taming the Tongue

We need to be careful about what we say. Outspoken people can do a lot of harm. Where there are two or more opposing sides, the view we choose to promote needs to be right. In 2021, all over the world, there was opposition to the coronavirus vaccine. So many different ideas were put forward. Medical authorities said one thing and other groups of people said another. Which one was right? Does there have to be a right or wrong? If we choose to be the person who speaks on behalf of others, can we be sure we are on the right track? Can we control our urge to say something before we have the right answer? It is good that some people are willing to be a voice for others.

Throughout history, there have been so many very brave people who have spoken out against something wrong. The story has been told and made into a film of the German, Lutheran Pastor, Dietrich Bonhoeffer, who spoke out against Adolf Hitler and was eventually executed for voicing his opinion.

Some of our common problems relate to how we speak about others. Criticism comes easy to some, while others see the best in people. According to this Bible reading, the important part is to allow God to run a check on us.

It can be depressing if we dwell too much on our failures, and we all have them, so looking to God's Holy Spirit to tame our tongue is a good way to go.

The art of speaking God's word in public places, on street corners or in parks has probably given way to the modern media stage. Wherever and whenever we take our stand and proclaim something, it is good if it is God's word at the right time. The Holy Spirit can empower us to bring good news and Godly wisdom to those who want to hear.

"Lord God, thank you for giving us the courage to speak up. Please tame our tongues and help us to speak wisely and with respect for others. Thank you, Jesus."

James 3:2, 8, 9
We all stumble in many ways. If anyone is never at fault in what he says, he is a perfect man, able to keep his whole body in check. V.8 But no man can tame the tongue. V.9 With the tongue we praise our Lord and Father, and with it we curse men, who have been made in God's likeness.

'Just a Reminder-Each Day'

March 16

A Home with a View

We live in a 'Lucky Country', or we could say a 'God Favoured Country'. Most people have a home and whether it is a rental, shared home or owned, it is probably not a pile of sticks lent together or a tent in a refugee camp. Most Australians know they live in a favoured country, but where we live and how we live do not always go as planned. The desire to have a home with a view has led to some nasty relationships between owners, neighbours and the local council. It seems that any rules set up to protect those living on the second street back, or even further, from losing their view, don't always work. Sometimes decisions are made that ignore the rights of others. We have plenty of wonderful views in our country, especially along the coast and around the hills.

It is not a popular truth, but according to the Bible, humankind is basically selfish. If we are honest, we will admit that we want a home with a view and even if it doesn't suit the house behind us, we may just go ahead anyway.

Jesus had a similar situation when two of his followers wanted a guarantee that one of them would be given a seat on the left and the other a seat on the right of him when he began his reign. They wanted the house with a view! Jesus tried to tell them that it wasn't going to be as glamorous as they thought. There was no way they could have understood what Jesus was about to go through.

There is nothing wrong with wanting a house with a view or a place of honour, but it is how we get there, what attitude we have and what actions we take, that count. Being humble may only mean, being open to God's direction rather than forging ahead without considering his way.

"Lord God, please help us with our selfish attitudes and actions. Thank you Holy Spirit for leading us into the truth, for guiding us in a better direction. Please help people to avoid conflict with a neighbour, council, or friends. Thank you, Jesus."

Matthew 23:12
For whoever exalts himself will be humbled, and whoever humbles himself will be exalted.

March 17
Pace Yourself

A woman turned up at a working bee, a little flustered from trying to get to the event on time. She was eager to do her share of the work, which she did, but she probably would have coped better if she had paced herself. 'Pace yourself' is a common enough term. Long-distance swimmers and runners know they must pace themselves to finish first. The jockeys who ride in the Melbourne Cup would be given clear instructions on how to pace their horse to complete the long-distance race successfully.

Whenever a big project or an event with a large time frame, is being worked through, people need to pace themselves rather than wear out. Anxious, exhausted people need to know when to ask for help. They need to know when to step back, take a break, delegate jobs and how to get fit for the journey, but more importantly, they need the Holy Spirit of God to pace them. We can all do better with his guidance.

I must admit I have often failed to pace myself while running camps and have ended up tired and hard to live with. One day when I was trying to get several things working at our youth camp, I sensed the Lord saying to me, 'Ask Trevor to do that job'. I quickened my steps and caught up to him. As Trevor and I walked towards the dining area, I presented the job to him and without hesitation, he agreed to do it. Of course, God knew that Trevor would go on from being a helpful young camper to marrying a woman with a similar vision, raising a family and taking on leadership roles in their home church. God had a plan for his life.

When we lose our peace and become anxious with those around us, we may need to ask for help and take time out to let the Holy Spirit reset our course.

"Lord God, I am so grateful to you for showing me how to pace myself. Your Holy Spirit is our best guide and helper. Thank you, Jesus,".

2 Thessalonians 2: 16
May our Lord Jesus Christ himself and God our Father, who loved us and by his grace gave us eternal encouragement and good hope, encourage your hearts and strengthen you in every good deed and word.

March 18

So Clever

What a wonderful world of people we are, so clever, capable, inventive, progressive and inspiring. There is hardly anything we can't do! This ideal is fine until we come across a problem we can't solve by ourselves. Even minor problems can beat us.

A grandfather happened to mention how energetic his grandchild was. Almost out of control, he admitted. This brings us back to reality. The fact is that as clever as we humans are, there will always be problems we're not sure how to fix. Human nature, the way children behave, for example, is challenging enough. Harsh discipline can turn the child away and cause them to become rebellious. Intense love for children and the fear of losing their confidence often prevent parents from disciplining enough. There must be a better way.

Who cares enough to help us? Who understands our human failings? Who is clever enough to fix them? Who knows the formula for success? The answer to all these scenarios should be God. He who fashioned humanity in his image should know us and our problems better than we know ourselves.

"Lord God, we have been raising children since Adam was a boy, but the magic formula for success isn't obvious. Please help us in all our negotiations with family, friends and other people. Help us to pray for

them and to recognise your influence in their lives and ours. Thank you, Jesus."

Hosea 11: 1-4
"When Israel was a child, I loved him, and out of Egypt I called my son. But the more I called Israel, the further they went from me. They sacrificed to the Baals, and they burned incense to images. It was I who taught Ephraim to walk, taking them by the arms; but they did not realise it was I who healed them. I led them with cords of human kindness, with ties of love, I lifted the yoke from their neck and bent down to feed them".

Deception or Harmless Fun

My mother took delight in telling me of the adventures that she and her young adult friends had on their interstate polocrosse trips. A team of six players had travelled interstate for a weekend tournament. There was more than polocrosse played on those weekends! One evening the visiting players wandered into a private party, hoping the host would be friendly and allow them to join in. When asked where the group came from, one of the players answered, 'Maitland'. With a gasp and look of sympathy, the host and other local guests began to ask the visitors questions about how they had survived the flood. The news of terrible floods in Maitland N.S.W. had been broadcast all over the nation. It became a case of mistaken identity, but the players decided to keep the truth to themselves for a while. The temptation to enjoy the attention and food and drinks on offer was strong. They avoided telling the host that they were from Maitland S.A.

After partying for a while, they admitted they were not victims of a flood, much to the hostess's relief. They expressed their gratitude for the hospitality and wandered back to their accommodation. Many laughs were had along the way and the story was told more than once when they returned to their home state. Other funny stories from similar trips away were always good for a laugh.

The deception was harmless, I guess, but deception with wrong motives can lead to some very unhappy results.

"Lord God, help us to have a good understanding of what is deception with wrong motives and what is harmless fun. Please help us to be true to you and honest in our dealings with people. Thank you, Jesus."

Galatians 6:7
Do not be deceived; God cannot be mocked. A man reaps what he sows.

'Just a Reminder-Each Day'

March 20
Swans

I t was a nice sunny day as we drove through a small country town leading to the causeway. I eagerly cast my eyes left and right. My mother was deliberately driving slowly across the bridge. I couldn't wait to see the black swans. My mother always reminded me to look out for them. Their long necks caught my attention as I counted three, maybe four or five, majestic birds floating on the shallow water that came in from the sea. A long narrow creek led into a small lake where ducks swam among the swans. It was a real treat in my childhood to see those graceful birds.

The Peninsula where I have always lived has neither mountains nor rivers, forests or freshwater lakes, but it does have lovely beaches, sandhills, surf and impressive rugged cliffs. The black swans always seemed to be a rare sight because the only other place we would see such elegant birds was on the river around our capital city, over 100ks away.

The things that impress us as a child often hold a special place in our hearts. The way we were taught and the values that shaped our lives stay with us. It can be difficult if our childhood attitudes and values need to change. Finding God or adjusting our views on faith can intercept our lives at any time. I am grateful to my mother for encouraging and nurturing my love of animals. It has been a good part of my life, but at a certain point in time, I had to make room for God. I needed to adjust and discover how to live with my old values and interests in a new way.

"Lord God, thank you for wonderful childhood memories. Please help us if our old values and attitudes need adjusting to your will for us. Thank you, Jesus."

Proverbs 3: 1-3
My son do not forget my teaching, but keep my commands in your heart, for they will prolong your life many years and bring you prosperity. Let love and faithfulness never leave you; bind them on your neck, write them on the tablet of your heart.

'Just a Reminder-Each Day'

March 21
Control

I have ridden horses most of my life and have usually felt in control. The exception to this came one day when my dog came racing across the paddock to catch up to me. The horse I was riding bolted! I had never had the misfortune of being on a bolting horse before. It was extremely scary! At some point, you accept that you have no control. I would have been about ten metres into the bolt when I realised I had no way of changing the grip on my reins, no way of turning the horse, no way of altering his speed - he was almost at full gallop and there was no way of getting off safely. I did the only thing I could do, and that was to hold on! I had no control! Eventually, the dog managed to get ahead of us. The horse slowed down; his heart was pounding, I could feel it and mine was, too. I was sure this horse had been frightened badly by dogs before I owned him and this day proved how terribly scared he was. I was not cross with him; just glad the Lord had taken care of both of us. I was able to avoid it ever happening again.

In human relationships, some people take control, consciously or subconsciously. A reaction to feeling intimidated by someone is to try and control them. This can happen in governing, business dealings, sports or friendship groups, too. We may not know we are doing it or that it is happening to us. It also happens in people's relationship with God. We may want to fully trust him, but just to be on the safe side, we exercise some level of control by keeping the relationship at a safe distance. God graciously offers unconditional love regardless of how we relate to him. If we recognise his unconditional love for us, we may find we can fully trust him.

Children and adults who have experienced domestic violence, or any other relationship breakdown, often react by keeping a tight rein on their feelings and relationships.

"Lord God, you offer us love and understanding even when we are holding on too tight to the reins of our lives. Please help us to trust you without needing to be in control. Thank you, Jesus."

Psalm 32: 9,10
Do not be like the horse or the mule, which have no understanding but must be controlled by bit and bridle or they will not come to you. Many are the woes of the wicked, but the Lord's unfailing love surrounds the man who trusts in him.

'Just a Reminder-Each Day'

March 22
Autumn is here

The strong winds have blown just about every leaf off the fruit trees, leaving them looking like skeletons. Only a day ago, they were green and full of life. Clouds cover the sky now as if it had never been blue. There is hardly any colour in the garden but at least the weeds haven't come up yet. Autumn can be gloomy. Life seems to have too many changes sometimes. Happy times just slip by and cannot be contained. God is supposed to be the same all the time; kind and caring, forgiving and faithful. So why are our lives always changing? Maybe it is good for us to have some undulation, happy times and sad times, a time to rejoice and a time to contemplate.

When I think about Autumn, I remember how much I love the season because it is usually calm, not too hot, cool but not cold. Autumn is my favourite season.

"Lord God, you created this world we live in with plenty of changes. Some we understand, and others we don't. Please help us not to be gloomy when things don't go our way; Instead, we ask for a positive, grateful heart to navigate the way through. Thank you, Jesus."

Malachi 3:6
I the Lord do not change.

Isaiah 54: 10
"Though the mountains be shaken, and the hills be removed, yet my unfailing love for you will not be shaken nor my covenant of peace be removed," says the Lord, who has compassion on you.

Methodical

Some people are very methodical in their ways. This can be annoying, or it can be helpful. My mother-in-law asked me what I had done to the fence. I could not understand what she was saying but then I realised it was the hedge that grew along the fence that she was referring to. I had trimmed the dwindling pink blooms and tidied up the hedge as its flowering season was over.

We are familiar with plants flowering in each season, grasses coming and going, the sky changing with each new weather pattern and temperatures dictating what we wear and what we do. But do we stop to think about what a methodical God we have? He has set up methods that we can follow. Many aspects of life are predictable because there is a method in them. I was watching a television program with interest as two men passed new sheets of corrugated iron from a ladder to the roof ready for nailing down. The sheets had to go on a certain way, so the first man passed each sheet facing the right way, to be received and placed straight onto the roof. They set up a method that worked.

Back in the 18th. Century John and Charles Wesley, along with George Whitefield, taught about God in a way that labelled them Methodist. 'Jesus Christ, the Son of God, died for all humanity and that salvation is available for all'. This led to a great revival in the Church of England.

The teachings that Methodists saw as the foundation of the Christian faith were:

1) People are all, by nature, 'dead in sin'.
2) They are justified by faith alone.
3) Faith produces inward and outward holiness.

God's method of salvation through Jesus for all people still turns people's lives around centuries later. In the Romans reading, Paul was making the point that God's method of salvation, 'Jesus giving his life for all mankind', justifies all who turn to him for all time.

"Lord God, your methodical way is something dependable we can hold onto. Thank you, Jesus."

Romans 5: 18
Consequently, just as the result of one trespass was condemnation for all men, so also the result of one act of righteousness was justification that brings life for all men.

'Just a Reminder-Each Day'

March 24

Canoes

Glorious sunshine highlighted the clear blue sea. As far as the eye could see, it glimmered, calm and shallow. The young people in their canoes had drifted further out than I cared to follow. Most of the other campers had returned over the small sand dune to the campsite. I wanted to call out, "Time to come in" but I knew the last group paddling around, talking and laughing, would not hear me. I stood on the beach wondering how important it was that I called them back, but the tranquillity and absolute beauty of that place held me spellbound. I was easily able to see them, even hear their happy voices and they probably didn't even notice me. I returned to camp, trusting God that they would come in soon enough. I was quite familiar with that beach, as it was part of the same bay where our Pony Club camps were held many years prior. The huge expanse of sand, when the tide is out, works well for horse riding. When the tide is in, it is equally suitable for canoeing, as the water remains shallow and calm for a long distance.

When he called Nathanael to follow him, Jesus admitted that he had seen him from a distance, sitting under a fig tree. The fact that Jesus knew things about this man and could see him, without being there, immediately rang true for Nathanael. It can do the same for us, too. Jesus is no ordinary man. The life he lived supported the statement that Nathanael made regarding him. People often need to have a glimpse of the miraculous, some sense of the divinity of Jesus before they can truly believe in him.

"Lord God, I thank you for the miraculous, the beauty of our beaches, the evidence that you are God. Thank you, Jesus."

John 1: 48,49
Jesus answered, "I saw you while you were still under the fig tree before Philip called you." Then Nathanael declared, "Rabbi, you are the Son of God; you are the king of Israel."

'Just a Reminder-Each Day'

March 25
Jonah and the Whale

A recent newspaper item told the story of a man who spent some time in the mouth of a whale before it spat him out. The man survived to tell the story. Christians get excited when they hear stories that give credibility to a Bible story like Jonah and the Whale. The possibility of a man surviving in the stomach of a whale for three days has been debated over the centuries. After Jesus had referred to the Jonah story (Matthew 12:40), he pointed out how Jonah's three days in the whale were like the Son of Man, who would be three days in the earth. Jesus was talking about his death. (Did Jesus already know how his death was going to play out? Wow!) When people get a diagnosis that gives them a limited time to live, quite naturally, they struggle to come to terms with it. It is very sad. Here we have Jesus telling of his own limited time on earth, but he powers on, telling his followers about God the Father and healing people as he went. The Pharisees, church leaders of the time, were stunned by the insight and knowledge Jesus seemed to have. It scared them and threatened their status as leaders, particularly when Jesus talked of God as if he knew him personally.

When we see how much Jesus was aware of God's plan for him, we become more confident that Jesus was God in person; how else would Jesus have known about his own death? People have searched for evidence of the Ark and some have been sure they have found sections of wood that must have belonged to it. Proof of God and

Bible stories, along with the quest to prove who Jesus was, will probably go on for eternity. With the help of the Holy Spirit and giving ourselves some time to read the Bible, we can gather these little treasures that build our faith and confidence in God. For me, this one sentence that reveals Jesus knew how he would die, well before the event, but continued teaching the thousands that followed him, tells me that he must have been a superhuman or he must be God.

"Lord God, please help us in our doubts and unbelief. Please help us to have more faith. Please help us to be able to read the Bible and have our eyes open to your truth. Lord, I want to know you more. Thank you, Jesus."

Romans 10:17
Consequently, faith comes through hearing the message and the message is heard through the word of Christ.

'Just a Reminder-Each Day'

March 26
Gifts

Riding at Pony Club was a big part of my childhood but when I became old enough I tried instructing my peers. I was surprised to find they enjoyed and benefitted from my ideas. It gave me huge pleasure. I enjoyed many years of instructing after I had outgrown being a riding member. At the time I didn't know that my ability to instruct was a gift from God, but I did know that it felt good to be able to pass on what I had learnt about riding and to see others benefit.

At one rally, I was instructing a group of young riders where one rider on a smart-looking black pony was having trouble keeping it under control. I offered a few words of advice each time he went past me, but it wasn't helping. A friend from the city who had been staying with us took the little rider aside to give him some special help. Now and then, I glanced away from my group to see how John was doing. I noticed him encouraging the young rider to sit stronger in his saddle. I realised he was helping him to get his shoulders back and keep his weight from being pulled forward by the pony. This enabled him to stay firm in his saddle, resulting in the pony submitting and relaxing.

I was impressed with John's instruction. I could see how effective the method was and how much happier the rider and pony were. No punishment had to be given to the pony to have good results. It was just a matter of empowering the rider and convincing the pony that it could conform and be happy.

The gifts that God gives us can empower us to live a more victorious life. Recognising and using our gifts will most likely lead us to help others more effectively, too.

"Lord God, thank you for the gifts you give us to use in many areas of life. Please help us to use them wisely. Thank you, Jesus."

James 1:17
Every good and perfect gift is from above, coming down from the Father-

March 27

Freestyle to Music

I could not believe I had drawn first. I was about to compete in an event I had only imagined competing in. I had no experience to draw from. My mother was so excited initially in the planning for this competition where her delightful, dependable horse could be shown. We would take her first cross Andalusian, El Paso and our second cross Andalusian, Mantaquillo, to compete in the National Andalusian Horse Association competition in our local city. My daughter was going to ride El Paso in the show jumping events and I would compete on him in the dressage. We exhibited both horses in the led classes. I had dreamed of one day riding a Free Style to Music Dressage Test but living in a small country town, the opportunity didn't exist. Going to the city was costly and a big step for us.

We had made it to the Nationals! I nervously trotted up to the judge at the Wayville Show Grounds, saluted and waited for my music to tell me when to enter the arena. Finding the right piece of music had been a strange experience as I knew nothing about music except what makes my foot tap and what sounds like it fits with the rhythm of a horse's hoof beats. I wasn't confident that my test would score well because I knew I was a real beginner in this field. I had ridden many ordinary dressage tests in my life, but this was different. I was rather shocked at my final salute to hear the crowd applauding. The exhilarating feeling of getting praise for what I had wanted to do for so long was as good as standing on the podium at the Olympic Games with a medal around my neck.

When I remember that special occasion, I realise what a wonderful life I've been given. I didn't need to win that event. Coming anywhere was fine because the thrill had been in competing, and being applauded was confirmation that it was good enough. So often, people who have attained something great say, "If I can do it, so can you" and of course that is not a well-thought-out statement. So many people don't have the opportunities, abilities, finance, support or even the health to reach the heights others have.

"Lord God, I thank you for all you have given me, including family, friends and opportunities at the right time and place. Thank you, Jesus."

1 Chronicles 16: 8
Give thanks to the Lord, call on his name; make known among the nations what he has done.

'Just a Reminder-Each Day'

Jet Trails

For some people, the thought of living in the country is a lonely thought, quite unappealing. Those of us who are happy in the country, where jet trails are easily seen decorating the sky, know we are not alone. We look up, wondering where the occupants of each jet are heading, where they came from and why they are flying today.

The sky has been used as a drawing board for all sorts of things like marriage proposals, air force displays, air ballooning and parachuting.

In the book of Daniel, some writing took place that would have had even the strongest of us shaking. Daniel had been imprisoned and virtually forgotten, but God had a great plan for him. He was called to interpret the writing on the wall. Daniel seemed fearless in the way he pointed out all the failings of the King's father and suggested that the King, too, had dishonoured God. Daniel was elevated to a high position because he was the only one able to interpret the writing. He could then do more of what God had planned for him.

"Lord God, please help us to respect and honour you and not take you for granted. Please uphold us with your mercy and love. Please keep writing messages for us, in the sky, on our door mats, in our minds and any time we read your word. Thank you, Jesus."

Daniel 5: 5,6
Suddenly the finger of a human hand appeared and wrote on the plaster of the wall, near the lampstand in the royal palace. The king

(Belshazzar) watched the hand as it wrote. His face turned pale, and he was so frightened that his knees knocked together, and his legs gave way. V.21b (Daniel led into his interpretation by saying) the most high God is sovereign, over the kingdoms of men and sets over them anyone he wishes. V. 26-28 (the interpretation of the writing on the wall) God has numbered the days of your reign and brought it to an end. You have been weighed on the scales and found wanting. Your kingdom is divided and given to the Medes and Persians.

‘Just a Reminder-Each Day’

March 29

Friends Earn Their Title

offered to help a woman who had been going through a difficult time. We weren't close friends, but I was surprised when she declined my offer, saying she had friends and they were very supportive. 'Ouch! O K.' I thought I had done the right thing because sometimes Christians and the church receive some bad press for not being there for people when support is needed.

On reflecting, I realised we don't suddenly become someone's friend. We earn the title of 'friend' through our consistent friendship. We need to be there for each other through the good and bad times and sometimes make sacrifices for each other. Wanting to take God to people when we think they are in need isn't that easy. Discerning God's direction and wanting earnestly to be helpful is important.

Maybe if I had just started the conversation by showing I cared, it would have been more appreciated. Then there are other occasions when going in full of confidence is just what the receiving person needs. I am grateful that the lady does have good friends.

"Lord God, please help us to get it right! Help us to understand your will on each individual case where we feel led to offer help. Thank you, Jesus."

John 15: 15
I no longer call you servants, because a servant does not know his master's business. Instead I have called you friends, for everything I learned from my father I have made known to you.

Proverbs 17: 17
A friend loves at all times.

March 30
Even the Dogs

Walking along the garden path, I kicked a tin can instead of picking it up; I was mad! The day had turned out differently than I had planned and now I had to do something I didn't want to do. I complained to God and I complained to my husband and then I sulked. I continued complaining while I was cleaning the windows.

I thought the dog should be happy with my company as I moved the ladder from one window to the next, but she looked like she was sulking, just like me. I guess she wished we would either go to the beach or the farm or at least go somewhere. Then I thought of the story where a woman was bold enough to tell Jesus what she believed. The woman stated her rights, but she also stated what she believed to be a dog's right (to have the crumbs from under the table).

My thoughts went to other dogs, the ones that never get taken anywhere and those that get ill-treated, but I also thought of how happy our working dogs were when they had spent hours working sheep. They would return to the house with us at the end of the day and then flop on the back mat, tired and totally satisfied with their day. They were well-fed and had comfortable beds. Most dogs seem happy and satisfied with their lot in life if they have the essentials like food, shelter, love and stimulation.

In the story, the woman with Jesus received all she wanted from him when her daughter was healed.

"Lord God, thank you for hearing us when we are stressed and in need of a good listening ear. Thank you, Jesus."

Matthew 15: 22-27
A Canaanite woman from that vicinity came to him (Jesus), crying out, "Lord, Son of David, have mercy on me! My daughter is suffering terribly from demon possession." He answered, "I was sent only to the lost sheep of Israel." The woman came and knelt before him, "Lord, help me!" He replied, "It is not right to take the children's bread and toss it to their dogs." "Yes Lord", she said, "but even the dogs eat the crumbs that fall from their master's table."

'Just a Reminder-Each Day'

March 31

Crouch Don't Run

Walking home from the stables I noticed one of our cats waiting on the pathway for me but immediately behind me, I heard the thundering sound of our sheepdog catching up. She continued flat out past me and straight past the cat. The wise cool cat had crouched down but didn't shy away from the dog. The thought went through my mind "How can a cat trust a dog?"

In this case, our dog and the cat have grown up together. They played together as a pup and a kitten, so the cat holds firm to the truth that the dog has no intentions of harming him. That works provided the cat doesn't lose confidence and decides to run, then the dog may be tempted to chase the cat.

How do we trust God when danger looms - can we hold onto the promise that he will never leave us? It is in trusting instead of running that we discover how faithful and trustworthy God is. Many people give up on God. For them, it seems easier to move away rather than hang in there. The 'crouch don't run' concept looks too hard.

There is nothing wrong with crouching in the face of danger, but running attracts attention and we become vulnerable. It is a fact that if you want to go unnoticed you are better off remaining perfectly still rather than risk moving.

"Lord God, please help me to crouch in your arms rather than run when trouble threatens me. I want to hold on to you, not lose confidence. Please supply me with enough faith to stay firm in the truth that you can be trusted. Thank you, Jesus."

Proverbs 3: 5
Trust in the Lord with all your heart and lean not on your own understanding.

   'Just a Reminder-Each Day'

Misjudging

The beginning of a camp always has an element of uncertainty. All the preparation has been done but the results are in the daily life of the camp. Often, I have names of people in my books who I do not know. Some of the registrations that come in I recognise from other years and some are new to me. The first night is awkward for the campers and even for the organisers; it has a strange feeling of being unknown. We may have organised many camps before, but the settling-in process still has us a little on edge. I noticed a girl laughing and relating to some of the campers as if she had always been at our camps, but I knew she hadn't. One of the other organisers whispered to me, "Who's that girl," I smiled and said I didn't know.

As the camp progressed, I worked out who the girl was, but her over-friendly, confident way intimidated me. I was used to campers feeling a little apprehensive until they settled in, but to have someone confident without any warmup time was unusual. Strangely, I felt I couldn't trust her, although she wasn't presenting as untrustworthy. During the camp, I found out more about this girl and managed to accept her. It wasn't until the following year, when the same girl came to camp again, that I realised I had misjudged her.

During the year, I got to know her as a genuine Christian girl with a happy, outgoing nature, gifts and a willingness to fill many roles. It didn't take long for all of us in the leadership team to welcome this new young lady with open arms. We grew to appreciate her immensely.

The Pharisees misjudged Jesus too. They saw his confidence in God as a threat and looked for ways to bring him down. Jesus was the genuine real Son of God, but they didn't get it. Misjudging someone can be a waste of time.

"Lord God, I thank you for the people who have proven to be wonderful friends even if I have misjudged them at first. Please help me to be a better judge of people. Thank you, Jesus."

Romans 2: 1
You, therefore, have no excuse, you who pass judgment on someone else, for at whatever point you judge the other, you are condemning yourself because you who pass judgment do the same things.

Sacrifice

In organising youth camps, I know some things need to be in place for the camp to run smoothly. Kitchen staff, games organisers, MC, music team and leaders for night duty are essential. In the lead-up to some camps, I have been quite concerned when it seemed we would be short-staffed. That would lead to phone calls and a lot of praying. If I failed to recruit enough helpers, I knew the camp would be more work than pleasure. In other years we would be well supported.

One year a married couple came but they were unsure what their role would be. We soon realised how valuable these people were in many areas of camp life. Since that first year, they have continued to be loyally involved. Recently, the wife announced, about one month before camp, that her elective surgery for her knee would be available about two weeks before camp and she was unsure if she would still be on crutches or any help at all for camp. I saw true faithful sacrifice in action on the first night of camp as she hobbled in on her walking stick and helped with the registration and directing of campers. I knew she was in pain, but her involvement was needed and so appreciated. She spent the rest of the time at home recovering while her faithful husband continued to work at camp each day.

Jesus talked to his disciples about walking the extra mile and giving the shirt off their backs. My friend certainly demonstrated how to give as much as could be given. The Spirit of God seems to inspire some people to take up causes, to do that extra bit and to strive for His will to be done. Thanks, M & C.

"Lord God, we thank you for all the kind and sacrificial things people have done for us. Help us to recognise these acts and show gratitude. Thank you, Jesus."

Romans 12: 6-8
We have different gifts according to the grace given us. If a man's gift is prophesying, let him use it in proportion to his faith. If it is serving, let him serve; if it is teaching, let him teach; if it is encouraging, let him encourage; if it is contributing to the needs of others, let him give generously, if it is leadership, let him govern diligently; if it is showing mercy, let him do it cheerfully.

The Power of Faith

Our involvement in running youth camps has taken us through various situations. There were times when the scales were tipped against us and times when the scales were tipped in our favour. In the years when many of the campers were from unbelieving homes, it seemed we were always working uphill to help them focus on getting to know Jesus. We battled against unbelief and unruly behaviour. The campers from Christian homes were outnumbered by those who didn't really understand what we were talking about. This went on for many years, but gradually, at some stage, the scales tipped in favour of us. Some of the young campers who found faith in Jesus became strong leaders. Instead of dropping out of camps when they grew older, they kept coming back, and their leadership turned camps around. The atmosphere of little faith became one of great faith. This change took the weight off our shoulders. The camps were much easier to run. We realised these new leaders were praying for God to do great things, and he did.

There can be an unbalance in our homes, work or any place where unbelief outweighs belief in Jesus. Our prayer was that God would allow us to have more young people become strong in their faith. We can pray that for any situation, not just for personal areas but for governments, too. Our testimony is that people, especially young people, who rely on God for guidance manage life better. God makes a difference.

"Lord God, you know what a battle it is when so few people acknowledge you. Please change our circumstances so that faith in you and your power shows up in governments, schools, universities, law enforcement, medical systems, communities and our families. Let us honour you as our sovereign leader. Thank you, Jesus."

Hebrews 12: 1,2
Therefore, since we are surrounded by such a great cloud of witnesses, let us throw off everything that hinders and the sin that so easily entangles, and let us run with perseverance the race marked out for us. Let us fix our eyes on Jesus, the author and perfector of our faith, who for the joy set before him endured the cross, scorning its shame, and sat down at the right hand of the throne of God.

                    'Just a Reminder-Each Day'

April 4
Tolerance

Our small country church showed great tolerance towards us in the days of our youth group. We were trying out our newfound theology. We played modern songs but sang with little understanding of the faith we were promoting. We needed an audience to practice on and our congregation excelled in that area.

We were motivated by the movement of God's Holy Spirit to conduct youth services of worship with enthusiasm. Although we were carried along by the spiritual revival of the time, it did not mean we had a good understanding of God or had any special insight to share with our congregation. Their tolerance gave room for us to grow.

It was an exciting time of learning, being challenged, inspiring each other and, most of all, experiencing God as we had never experienced before. We wrote plays and acted out our faith, broke down barriers and tested the boundaries, and still, the congregation showed tolerance and acceptance of us. They were encouraging and supportive.

"Lord God, we thank you for the tolerance others have shown to us. Thank you for your patience and tolerance surpassing understanding. Thank you, Jesus."

But what does it matter? The important thing is that in every way, whether from false motives or true, Christ is preached. And because of this I rejoice. Yes, and I will continue to rejoice.

Wedding Planning

As the date grew closer for our daughter's wedding, people began offering to help. I was very grateful when a friend offered to do the flower arrangements for the church, which certainly is not an area of my expertise. Whenever the wedding topic came up, more friends offered to do things like table arrangements, catering, music and setting up the hall. Our son-in-law's family loved being involved wherever they could. Our daughter did an amazing amount of the preparations herself, but as a family, we appreciated all the help that was being offered.

Many wedding jobs can only be done the day before and some on the wedding day, so when we discussed how we would decorate the bridal table and if flowers could be laid along the edge the night before, the lady who supplied us with the impressive dark red gladioli gave us the instructions on how to keep them looking fresh.

197

Each person who offered to do something added to the wedding day, making it a very happy event. In so many ways in life, the support of others completes our experience. In our desire to be helpful, it is good if we can see where we slot in, not presuming to do everything but knowing where we are most valued.

"Lord God, we are very grateful for the people who happily help us when the event is big or difficult. Please help us to understand the roles in which we work most effectively. Please guide us by your Holy Spirit to know where and when we can help others. Thank you, Jesus."

1 Corinthians 12: 4
There are different kinds of gifts, but the same Spirit. There are different kinds of service, but the same Lord. There are different kinds of working, but the same God who works all of them in all men.

'Just a Reminder-Each Day'

April 6
Transformed

We gathered our school lunch boxes and wandered down to the bank of the lake. It was nice on the only patch of lawn in the schoolyard, and now that we were year eight students, we were choosing to sit and talk over our lunch instead of rushing off to play. We knew we were maturing!

The four-day Easter holiday had been a nice break from school. Some of the girls talked about their weekend experience but the most interesting story was told by our usual out-spoken, often crude-speaking, most entertaining classmate. I liked her even though she embarrassed me occasionally with her brazen ways. If the teacher left the room, she would take the opportunity to tell dirty jokes and hold everyone's attention until the teacher returned.

She quietly unwrapped her sandwich and started to tell us about her Easter Camp adventure. Unlike her usual way of holding our attention, she politely described the camp run by Christians and how it had been a very happy time for her. I barely heard a word she said, her whole attitude had changed and that had me transfixed on her. I couldn't believe what I was hearing and who it was who was telling the story. I must admit I considered myself quite grown up, but I never questioned why she had changed. It wasn't until many years later when I had experienced the saving power of Jesus in my life, did I understand what had happened to my classmate. I often wonder why I didn't think more deeply about her transformation. I wasn't aware that people could change or even be changed by God.

"Lord God, I am so glad you took me from my shallow thinking and showed me how to believe in you and see life from a different perspective. Thank you, Jesus."

2 Corinthians 5: 17
Therefore, if anyone is in Christ, he is a new creation; the old has gone, the new has come!

‘Just a Reminder-Each Day’

April 7
Freely

I t is a good sign that in our small country town, the conservative Uniting Church and the Pentecostal Light Church are combining for some of their services. The differences are not so obvious now, and the hospitality and friendship shared between the groups are very enjoyable.

After one such church service, I wandered up to the coffee counter where a good friend was on duty to serve coffee. I had the correct money ready when his friendly voice called to me over the top of the happy chatter, "It's free today." I hesitated, trying to process what he had said, while he repeated, "It's free today; the coffees are free!" My thoughts had darted back to the last time we visited their church and how it turned out to be a free meal, so I wanted to give something back. I reached out with my money, ready to suggest it could be a donation, but again my friend tried to get through to me, "It's free because we left the money till home!" Oh! Now I was getting it! A bit slow! I accepted the free coffee and passed one to my husband while smiling apologetically at my friend who was busy making another coffee.

Talking over the incident with my husband later, he pointed out how difficult it is to do something contrary to our culture and added, 'You get what you pay for.' This thought took me to the Bible verse about receiving freely. We need to accept, receive and take with gratitude those things in life that are freely given to us especially God's gift of eternal life. It is not just salvation that God offers freely, but also day-to-day support, healing, advice, power to overcome our enemies and the list goes on. To follow that up, we can respond by sharing our story of faith in Jesus.

"Lord God, I accept all that you want to give me. Help me to pass on what I have to others. Thank you, Jesus."

Matthew 10: 7,8
As you go preach this message; 'The kingdom of heaven is near.' Heal the sick, raise the dead, cleanse those who have leprosy, drive out demons. Freely you have received, freely give.

Well done!

How hard is it to please God? We understand pleasing people. Manners and being helpful are taught to us from an early age. At some stage in our lives, we become aware of what it takes to please someone else. Gratitude was welling up in me on our return home from another horse competition. I had been successful enough to be bringing home a ribbon or two. I thanked my husband for his usual support. I thought about my mother and how her support had contributed to the day and, unconsciously, I appreciated our children for their happy attitude even when their mother was having most of the fun.

The big events on the farm were times when our family could be supportive and I knew the more we did to help prepare for harvest, seeding and shearing, the more grateful my husband was.

We can be obsessed with pleasing people, or we can completely overlook others and think only of ourselves. Somewhere there needs to be a balance.

Our involvement in running youth camps each Easter has revealed to me, sometimes as a pleasant surprise, how helpful people can be when they are most needed. From the time our children were able to fold and staple programs, to becoming adults who checked lights and tyres on the caravan and helped to pack our huge cargo to take to camp, we have been blessed. Nephews and nieces, friends from around the corner, neighbours up the road (minding our dogs while we were at camp), parents and other friends had done so much when we needed support.

"Lord God, we are so grateful when someone turns up unexpectedly to lend a hand. Thank you for all those people who have responded to your prompting, consciously or unconsciously, and lightened our load. Thank you, Jesus."

Matthew 10: 40-42
If anyone gives even a cup of cold water to one of these little ones because he is my disciple, I tell you the truth, he will certainly not lose his reward.

'Just a Reminder-Each Day'

April 9
99 Cat

This is a sad story, so if you are sensitive about animals, you may want to brace yourself first, but please read on. I am sure you won't regret it.

I wandered through the tall grass with my spray unit. While feeling glad I had made a start before the snakes came out of hibernation and the weeds got too tall, my eyes caught a glimpse of our cat called 99, hidden in tall grass. The denseness of the grass made me realise it was a miracle that I even saw her. She meowed at me as I bent down, and it was then that I realised my dear tortoiseshell cat was seriously injured. I picked her up and made my way back to the house. As I studied her injuries, she lay quiet in my arms as she had done many times over her long life. So bad were her injuries that I knew very quickly I was on a mercy mission to have her put out of her suffering. I started to thank the Lord out loud. "Thank you, Jesus," I said as I realised he had given me the chance to hold my cat and say goodbye, but more than that, I was able to shorten her suffering. I was convinced the Lord had taken me directly to this cat to rescue her.

It was not the first time I had rescued 99. She was just the cutest kitten but she had been abandoned. I coaxed her out of hiding with food, wrapped a jumper over her and quickly got her into our car and home. 99 grew up to be a fun cat. On the day of our daughter's wedding, we had a small group of people, including the bride and her bridesmaids, having photos taken on the farmyard lawn. 99 saw the opportunity to run under the wedding dress. It was too much fun to turn down. She ran in and out, patting at the hem and amusing us greatly. The photographer was concerned that the kitten would mess up the photos, but I assured him that a kitten peeping out from under a wedding dress would be a unique photo. 99 had a long and happy life on the farm, so I was sure this was not a time for being distressed but rather for being grateful to my God for taking care of her final hour.

"Lord God, we thank you for our pets. Thank you for being very much aware of the needs of all living creatures. Thank you, Jesus."

Genesis 1: 26
Then God said, "Let us make man in our image, in our likeness, and let them rule over the fish of the sea and the birds of the air, over the livestock, over all the earth, over all the creatures that move along the ground."

April 10

Gold Handled Knife

Early planning and visual effects will often tell us how important an event is. For example, anyone who has organised a wedding knows that the bride and groom and their families will pay a lot of attention to the details. Preparing for our daughter's wedding, when the big details had been taken care of, we realised we needed a knife for the 'cake cutting'. My mother offered to take care of that small detail, and the results were good. An ordinary knife was transformed into an elegant, gold glitter-handled knife with a gold ribbon attached. Marriage between a man and woman is usually treated as an important celebration, a commitment between two people that will affect the rest of their lives.

During a time of Spiritual revival in the 1970s- 80s, we regularly attended the Charismatic Conventions in Adelaide. The venue, with more rows of seating than could be counted at a glance and people to usher the crowds in, gave an air of excitement. The atmosphere represented the faith and expectations of the organising churches. People by the thousands streamed into the Show Ground Pavilion, coming from all over the state and interstate, with various reasons for attending. Some came because they had been invited by friends, other people wanted to see something big of God and some were just curious. A band led the crowd in soul-stirring songs, followed by a well-publicised and much-anticipated speaker. Dignitaries were given an opportunity to speak to the crowd. The evening was detailed to impress and win people to have faith in God. It was an atmosphere where God was present. People wanted more of Him!

When we want these events to be special, inviting God to bless them should result in lasting good memories.

"Lord God, thank you for the examples you have given us of how and what we need to celebrate. Thank you, Jesus."

Exodus 12: 26
And when your children ask you, 'What does this ceremony mean to you?' then tell them, 'It is the Passover sacrifice to the Lord, who passed over the houses of the Israelites in Egypt and spared our homes when he struck down the Egyptians.' Then the people bowed down and worshipped.

'Just a Reminder-Each Day'

April 11
A Loop in the Lead!

"That's been a long time coming," I told my dog. I wondered if I would ever see the day when she walked like other dogs, not pulling so hard on her lead that she almost choked herself. It has felt like a long journey of trying everything we could to get her to lead calmly. Many trips into the town for socialising while reassuring her, along with a lot of patience on our behalf, took place.

Life can include many such challenges. Raising children can seem like a long road, especially if they are over-active, rebellious or have ongoing health issues. Restoring something broken, building trust where trust is lost, getting through years of education, learning a new job or developing a new business can be a long journey with little ability to see what we will achieve in the end.

Training our young dog has been difficult. I think we have just taken it one day at a time, as people do when the road seems long and the end unsure. It is easy to be so intently focused on the immediate challenge that we do not even consider reaching our goal.

It was so rewarding to find our dog barely touching her lead. She has not completely matured, as she still pulls when something exciting happens but I can see she is making good progress.

When we are under pressure, consumed by a daily challenge, we need to have some peace to draw from.

Our God is faithful. We can lean on him each day, trusting he can get us through our immediate problems. Looking too far ahead can cause stress whereas daily trusting can give peace.

"Lord God, I ask for your encouragement and strength for other people who are struggling with daily challenges too heavy to carry alone. Please help them. Thank you, Jesus."

Psalm 28: 7
The Lord is my strength and my shield; my heart trusts in him, and I am helped. My heart leaps for joy and I will give thanks to him in song.

Yes or No

I t is obvious that some people procrastinate while others make quick decisions. Some deliberate briefly and, somehow, get it right. Not me! I jump in all too quickly, but because I am married to a man who takes his time weighing things up, I am persuaded to consider more carefully. This has probably helped me to make better decisions.

Jesus gave us much to think about with his Sermon on the Mount. His audience was challenged, advised and given directions that may have crossed over their cultural beliefs. He covered almost every subject on their minds at that time.

Don't swear by this or that, he told them. Just say what you think. In each culture, there are beliefs and traditions that people consider to be true and unchangeable. They are willing to swear by their religion, a person or a created idol. Jesus pointed out how inadequate this was. We have gone from swearing on oath in a law court using the Bible to being able to swear on the Koran or make an affirmation.

Adelaide Law School, Professor John Williams said swearing on the Bible had little meaning for people outside of the Christian faith. But he warned that adopting a uniform affirmation would not stop people from lying in court. In our current culture, it is common for someone to say, "I give you my word."

Jesus wants us to see that God the Father is the supreme authority and we are wise to honour him by speaking truthfully.

"Lord God, when it comes to knowing right from wrong and making decisions, please help us follow your leading; to be confident in your guidance. Thank you, Jesus."

Matthew 5: 37
Simply let your 'Yes' be 'Yes' and your 'No' be 'No'; anything beyond this comes from the evil one.

'Just a Reminder-Each Day'

April 13

The Long Drop

Some older people can still remember using the long drop. Life was very different then. A big hole in the ground covered by a wooden seat in a small wooden or corrugated iron shed just big enough for an adult to walk in, turn around, sit down, and walk out the door when the job was done, was the normal toilet. Most long drops were about 20 metres from the house, not so much fun going there in the dark. These quaint little buildings often housed spiders and small lizards, and on rare occasions, a snake may be found there. Regardless of the unwelcome wildlife, it was still a place for contemplation and meditation.

The modern indoor toilet certainly takes the prize for comfort but it lacks the character of the outside one. It doesn't have a view outside, wind noises, extreme temperatures or the occasional visit from a cat or dog just wanting a pat, but it, too, can be a place for contemplation and meditation.

Tractor driving, sheep droving on horseback, fishing on calm water, wandering in the garden or staring at the stars can take some beating for contemplation and meditation.

It doesn't matter where we spend time thinking when we invite God to direct our thoughts. His Holy Spirit may reveal some surprising ideas for us to follow, or we may find we have discovered more about God in that time.

"Lord God, please make yourself known to us in our quiet times. Please help us to discover more about you and your involvement in this world. Thank you, Jesus."

Psalm 8:3-9
When I consider your heavens, the work of your fingers, the moon, and the stars, which you have set in place, what is man that you are mindful of him, the son of man that you care for him? You made him a little lower than the heavenly beings and crowned him with glory and honour, you made him ruler over the works of your hands; you put everything under his feet: all flocks and herds and the beasts of the field, the birds of the air and the fish of the sea, all that swim the paths of the seas. O Lord, our Lord, how majestic is your name in all the earth.

April 14

The Keys

From a distance, I noticed a vehicle parked by the curb. It had chosen a park to accommodate the boat and trailer it was towing. One of the occupants came walking back to the vehicle and, when he was about two metres from his companion, threw what looked like a bunch of keys. The other man caught them and both got into the vehicle and drove away.

I thought 'Typical blokes, rather than having hand contact, throwing the keys is what you do.'

Which then made me think a little more deeply about contact. We Australians don't make physical contact with each other as much as some cultures do. But in saying that, I also realise we have changed. Thanks to television and travel, we see in some sports how different cultures go for the big embrace after a goal is scored. They embrace, and celebrate any achievement more than we do, but I think we have begun to copy them. Good or bad, I'm not sure, but sometimes it seems a shame to lose some of our cultural identity.

Embracing is a good thing. We humans need genuine touch, just like some animals do. There is room for people who shy away from embracing to try to embrace occasionally when the situation requires it and those who over-embrace need to respect the space others need.

Jesus, God's human representation of himself, grew up in a culture where embrace was a natural response in many situations. The Apostle Paul, in his letters to the new churches, tried hard to hold people together, to keep them focused in the right direction and to be outwardly supportive of each other, as seen in this bible reading.

"Lord God, please help us to show genuine love and support to each other. Thank you, Jesus."

2 Corinthians 13: 11,12, 14
Finally, brothers, good-bye. Aim for perfection, listen to my appeal, be of one mind, live in peace. And the God of love and peace be with you. Greet one another with a holy kiss. May the grace of the Lord Jesus Christ, God's love, and the Holy Spirit's fellowship be with you all.

April 15
Find a Way

had a growing uncomfortable feeling about smoking. I knew it wouldn't be easy if I decided to give it up after ten years. A guest speaker at church one Sunday told the story of how he received power from God to give up smoking. After having given it up for quite some time, he decided it would be all right if he took the habit up again because God would help him quit like he did the first time. This proved to be quite untrue as he found giving up this time almost impossible. He tried many times before eventually succeeding. He admitted that he felt God was not helping him the second time.

The story must have made an impression on me as a few days later I had a dream that God would give me a never-ending cold that would stop me from smoking. Some weeks later, travelling home from a dressage competition, my throat was sore. I felt so uncomfortable that I decided that having a cigarette was unappealing. I had forgotten about my dream. The next day I still felt so unwell that smoking wasn't an option. The days went on, my cold cleared up and I was able to leave the smoking alone. After the magic three weeks, I rejoiced at being free from the smoking addiction and gave God all the credit for helping me. What followed was a recurring dream where I found myself smoking again. I would wake up so disappointed until I realised it was only a dream. Those dreams, which eventually subsided, served me well to keep me free from returning to smoking—a real gift from God.

"Lord God, thank you for equipping us to overcome addictions and bad habits. Thank you for understanding our weaknesses and being willing to support us for a better outcome. Thank you, Jesus."

Psalm 18: 35
You give me your shield of victory, and your right hand sustains me; you stoop down to make me great.

'Just a Reminder-Each Day'

April 16
Terrible Twins (loyal friendships)

Two sweet-looking little blonde girls followed their mother around the supermarket. They were quiet and presented as well-behaved preschool-age children. While their mother was being served at the checkout, her sweet little twins quietly wandered off - so quietly that none of us noticed until the alarm went off. Then everyone near the checkout area turned and looked. The girls had tried to climb over or through the automatic opening gate and one seemed caught between the gate and a trolley. Neither of the girls looked worried. I wondered if they were used to getting into strange predicaments. On reflection, I also wondered if twins got into more mischief because they always had someone else there to take a risk with them. They may well become partners in crime at an early age! Just having a joke here, of course, but who we hang out with has some bearing on how we behave.

Some parents of teenage children encourage them to bring their friends home to their place so they know how they are being influenced. It means extra work and possibly a prayer or two, but it can pay off. The people we partner with in marriage, work, business, sport and many other areas of life can be good for us or lead us astray. Good partnerships have a lot going for them. Life can be really rewarding if the people we hang out with are good to learn from, appreciate our input into their lives, stimulate healthy discussion and inspire us to reach worthwhile goals. King David, in his youth, found a true friend in Johnathon. They inspired each other, stuck by each other in difficult circumstances and honoured God in the way they lived.

"Lord God, help us to be loyal in our relationships, a good influence on others and aware of your influence. Thank you, Jesus."

1 Samuel 18: 3,4
Jonathan made a covenant with David because he loved him as himself. Jonathan took off the robe he was wearing and gave it to David, along with his tunic and even his sword, his bow, and his belt.

'Just a Reminder-Each Day'

Body Language (Barriers up)

One year, Keith Urban, a judge on the television program 'The Voice', demonstrated to one of the contestants what he had experienced when doing gigs in Australian pubs. He folded his arms and expressed an attitude of judgement, saying words like, 'OK mate, show us what you can do,' and 'Come on then, can you sing or not,' showing the kind of reception he often encountered. He then changed his body language to hands hanging down by his side, saying this is how the audience looks when they have begun to accept you as an OK performer. He went on to suggest that a singer wants their audience to move into putting their hands in the air in praise of the performance.

This reminded me of a common attitude shown towards God. I can clearly remember how I felt when I first got involved with church, Bible studies and other Christian events; my arms were folded. I was apprehensive; I had my barriers up, as many people do. It's what we don't know about God that causes us to be wary. The sooner we realise God can be trusted, the more likely we will unfold our arms and give God some consideration.

God is the one we can fully trust. He is one hundred per cent in favour of us and doesn't approach us judgmentally. This is a truth all people need to know and experience.

"Lord God, thank you for accepting us as we are, blotches and all! Help us Lord to fully trust you, knowing that you have nothing but the best for us. Help us to be kind to the doubters and sceptics and to know how to nurture them to a place of acceptance and trust in you. Thank you, Jesus."

Romans 15: 13
May the God of hope fill you with all joy and peace as you trust in him, so that you may overflow with hope by the power of the Holy Spirit.

'Just a Reminder-Each Day'

Nothing goes Unnoticed.

Television and other forms of modern media allow us to see the headlines, the stories of those who are recognised for the good they have done, and their successes and failures. There are people we recognise who often have centre stage. Some are getting attention because they are our leaders, while others are temporarily in focus. There are other groups and individuals, often overlooked, who may wonder if anyone cares.

Soldiers returning from war, who faced death, lost mates and saw things they will never be able to forget, may wonder if anyone cares. Some young people give up their careers to care for a disabled parent. Other groups who may get overlooked are those who serve their community without receiving any rewards, single people who have missed out on marriage but continue to care for children, farmers and small businesses that work hard to make a profit and those who take second place without complaining.

It would be nice to be able to work for others or volunteer our time without expecting any acknowledgement, but our human nature usually demands a reward. When we feel that our effort has gone unnoticed, we need to turn to Jesus. He watches over us and fairly distributes his accolades to all who feel overlooked. No good deed or action goes unnoticed by our God.

"Lord God, please reassure those who feel unappreciated and help them to know that nothing they do goes unnoticed by you. Thank you for all the supportive people in our community who suffer silently and carry someone else's load. Thank you for the quiet achievers and those who are faithful in all they do without expecting something in return. Thank you, Jesus."

Psalm 139: 1
O Lord, you have searched me, and you know me. You know when I sit and when I rise; you perceive my thoughts from afar. You discern my going out and my lying down; before a word is on my tongue you know it completely, O Lord.

'Just a Reminder-Each Day'

Rehearsals

A singer, being interviewed on the radio, was asked if she was going to do any more concerts and, if so, what did she most look forward to. Her reply was "Rehearsals!" Immediately, I understood why she said that. Memories of a time when our Pony Club was rehearsing a musical ride sent some good feelings through me. Like most rehearsals, it was hard work. There were some tears and the occasional mess-up when a couple of riders ran into each other. However, most of the time it was heaps of fun! But it's the main event that counts.

Dressed in bright-coloured shirts, our Pony Club riders delighted their audience in a very unpretentious setting, in a scrub, miles from any town. They rode in circles, walked, trotted and cantered in single file, pairs and fours, weaving in and out of each other across the arena while the amplified music highlighted the graceful ride. The rehearsals had paid off.

Later in life, I had a similar 'good feeling' when our youth group prepared for events. The practising of plays often led to uncontrollable laughter. I was surprised by their acting ability and they even surprised themselves.

Jesus rode on a donkey into Jerusalem to the 'Main Event' of his earthly life. People cheered and waved palm branches, heralding Jesus as their hero. Pilate even asked Jesus if he was the Messiah. Jesus did not answer. He was on a mission to save the souls of people like you and me. He was heading for an unglorified death, not a crowning as his followers may have thought. The rehearsal seemed to have been the fun part of Jesus' life as he healed the sick and raised some from death. There was no fanfare at the cross! All seemed lost until Jesus rose from the dead three days later, and now we celebrate the risen Jesus thousands of years later.

"Lord God, we find ourselves almost speechless at how you chose to save mankind. Help us understand your life (the rehearsal), your death and resurrection (the main event), and what this means for us. Thank you, Jesus."

Luke 19: 35, 36, 37b
They brought it to Jesus, threw their cloaks on the colt and put Jesus on it. As he went along, people spread their cloaks on the road. The whole crowd of disciples began joyfully to praise God in loud voices for all the miracles they had seen.

'Just a Reminder-Each Day'

Sorry I Offended You

In some cases, it is easy to apologise to someone we have offended, and other times it is very hard. There are many circumstances in life where our conscience convicts us. When this happens, our first response should be to apologise, but we may not see that person again or even feel responsible for apologising. Other times, we may hurt someone more if we bring up the subject. Occasionally, what we thought was offensive may go unnoticed or even be overlooked. The

Jews were offended when Jesus forgave sins. *(Who does he think he is, going around forgiving sins? Matthew 9: 2-6)*

God is strong on forgiveness. The whole act of sacrifice, the son of God going to the cross willingly, is about God forgiving. If we offend one of God's children, we automatically offend God. Admitting our faults to God and asking for His forgiveness is liberating, and it is also empowering. We may not think we have the courage to apologise to someone we have offended but, with God's help, we can. What usually follows is that a great burden is lifted from our shoulders. Each time a relationship is mended, both parties are free to move on.

"Lord God, you know who and when I have offended. I pray for your healing in those people's lives. I ask for your forgiveness. Please mend all the relationships spoilt by my offensive behaviour or unwillingness to apologise. Thank you, Jesus."

1 John 1: 9
If we confess our sins, he is faithful and just and will forgive us our sins and purify us from all unrighteousness.

Push the Door

The door to understanding God seems hard to push open. So many people don't show any interest in finding God or are unaware that God has something to offer. The door appears blocked by complacency, lack of information and disillusionment, to mention a few.

Our streets don't have lions roaming ready to make a kill, neither are our houses being robbed while we sleep. Our country is not governed by a dictatorship that imprisons anyone who speaks their mind and gunmen don't lurk around each turn. Our fishing towns are not being washed away by tsunamis and the food-growing areas are not suffering decades of droughts. Children are not forced to work in mines and society is not banned from having religious beliefs; so, we're OK mate, we don't need God!

Basically, people are unsure if they need God or not. Christians may be uncertain about sharing their faith while the public may be unaware of the benefits of following Jesus.

All people have needs at some point and wonder who can help them; all Christians have a story to tell. Finding God comes in waves. Revivals are a testament to this. Those willing to introduce Jesus to another are often surprised at the reception. We don't know what God is doing and when he will be good news for someone.

At the church where we attend, the doors are often shut in the winter to keep the warm air in and on hot days to keep the building cool, but we understand this. We know that if we just push the door it opens easily and we are always welcome.

A sad part about going to church, or any Christian organisation, in this time where faith is not high on people's agenda, is that we must push the door open to find out what is on offer. Most people who push through are not disappointed.

"Lord God, you have so much to offer all of us; please help us to openly share our God experiences with people, so they don't have to push the door too hard to get to know you. Thank you, Jesus."

Luke 11: 9
So I say to you: Ask and it will be given to you; seek and you will find; knock and the door will be opened to you.

'Just a Reminder-Each Day'

✦

Will the Real Me Please Stand Up

A good friend once reassured me that being good with animals was still a good thing. As a relatively young Christian, I was becoming aware of the need to help people, but I found it hard and I continued to be drawn to the comfort of my animals. Spending time with animals alleviated the stress of relating to people. Her word to me was a good word at the right time. It made me feel better about myself. To be honest, I loved being with animals more than I loved being with people, except for the few very special people in my life. I had some growing to do as a Christian, but for that to happen, I needed some repair work to be done in my life.

The phrase 'finding ourselves' has been quite popular. It is as if some magic power to succeed is hidden in all of us. As a Christian, I am learning that God knows us better than we know ourselves. He is happy to reveal what he is already doing in us. We are more likely to find happiness and satisfaction when we discover ourselves in relationship to the One who created us.

Some people are naturally people-orientated, others are animal lovers and others are under-the-bonnet people. At the same time, some are sporty, arty, hands-on people and others are growers and builders. When it is all said and done, if God made us, then we are who he wants us to be, minus the faults!

"Lord God, thank you for the people who recognise the good you have done in us. Thank you for creating us uniquely different. Please help us to have your peace about ourselves and be comfortable with that. Thank you, Jesus."

Isaiah 64: 8
Yet O Lord, you are our Father. We are the clay, you are the potter; we are all the work of your hand.

'Just a Reminder-Each Day'

✦

April 23
Hidden

The shade cloth on our shade house had lifted a little in the earlier north wind, so I set myself up to do some mending; ladder, hammer, nails, a light timber batten to add to the roof and solid planks to walk on. It was an easy roof to access and with a view to admire. Perched up on the roof, after I had nailed the batten down at one end, I stopped to look around. The sea to the east was always a pleasant reminder of what a nice area we live in, and to the south, I could see right down over our farm. I went on hammering nails in, but something else caught my attention.

Three pairs of bright eyes were watching me from the tamarisk tree, so close to the shade house that I could study their every detail. If it wasn't for their enquiring, 'Why are you making that awful noise while we are trying to sleep?' stare, I would have missed seeing what was so amazingly hidden. Their speckled, greyish-fawn feathers resembled the coarse greyish bark on the tree, and their folded-down posture on the branch had them almost completely hidden. Disguised as a bulge in the branch, a family of Tawny Frog Mouths often referred to as Mopokes were huddled together. I tried to finish my hammering as quietly as I could and leave them to sleep. So many creatures can camouflage for their protection.

Jesus often talked to his followers in parables, the meaning hidden until disclosed. But the time had come for transparency, for the truth of God's plan to be clear to all who would hear. The

Jewish people knew God planned to send the Messiah and many prophetic words had been spoken to confirm it. But was Jesus the Messiah? It was as if God's secret plan was now being revealed, but not everyone could see it.

"Lord God, thank you for revealing your hidden plan to us, opening our eyes to see the truth and to know our Saviour. Thank you, Jesus."

Matthew 10: 26,27
There is nothing concealed that will not be disclosed or hidden that will not be known. What I tell you in the dark, speak in the daylight; what is whispered in your ear, proclaim from the roofs.

April 24

Fig Leaf

How far do we go, further than someone else? How far is far enough? The way women dress, particularly on reality television programs that play to the young audience, pushes the boundaries beyond belief. Women wear dresses with plunging necklines that barely leave anything to the imagination. These women often show signs of being uncomfortable wearing something too revealing that threatens to fall off their shoulders. It is possible that they have come under pressure to wear such outfits.

Surprisingly, this started with the fig leaf. Suddenly, Adam and Eve discovered that being naked was embarrassing. Apparently, when they walked with God in the garden, before they broke the rules, they were naked, in their birthday suits and not ashamed, just as God had made them.

Enter 'Sin' and an awareness of right and wrong, and the choice of pleasing God or ignoring him. We have come so far from the Garden of Eden that we have forgotten that the original offence was against God, and it still is.

The consequences of women's excessive exposure can be men misbehaving, disrespecting women, rape, domestic violence and sexual exploitation. It does not lead to God coming down and smacking us on the fingers; he doesn't need to because our foolish actions come back to bite us. We need to take responsibility for our actions, girls! Our extreme attempts to be admired can lead men to

235

think we are freely available and that we don't care what happens to our bodies, but we do!

If men hope to have good relationships with women, they can do the right thing by being proactive and resisting the temptation to think and talk about women's bodies. Stop before it gets out of hand! Sadly, some women make the mistake of exposing their bodies to get attention, when being discreet usually wins them long-term genuine friendships.

"Lord God, you are very patient with us, slow to get angry and always ready to forgive. Please help women to care for their bodies, and men respect them. Thank you, Jesus."

Ephesians 5: 8,9,10
For you were once darkness, but now you are light in the Lord. Live as children of light (for the fruit of light consists in all goodness, righteousness, and truth) and find out what pleases the Lord.

April 25
Guinea Pig Club

My mother's husband was a member of the Guinea Pig Club, which was formed during World War 11. He was a bombardier in the war when his plane was shot down and burst into flames, causing the occupants to be badly burnt. His face, and in particular his eyelids, were severely damaged. He spent a long time in the hospital unable to close his eyes. Many soldiers who suffered burns in the war were given skin grafts. This patchwork surgery was so

new that the patients were called Guinea Pigs. Although the work of those surgeons was nothing short of miraculous, Rhys bore the scars from the burns for the rest of his life, but he had a great attitude and appreciation for life.

When something new is offered to us, we have the opportunity to appreciate it or refuse it. Those WW11 soldiers would have accepted the pioneering work of skin grafting with gratitude as it gave so many of them hope for a normal life after the war.

"Lord God, thank you for all the amazing medical breakthroughs of our time. Thank you for new possibilities in our lives too. Please help us to try what you are offering and to trust you for the outcome. Thank you, Jesus."

2 Corinthians 4: 16
Therefore, we do not lose heart. Though outwardly we are wasting away, yet inwardly we are being renewed day by day.

✦

April 26
A Lasting Investment

People often ask us where we live since we moved from the farm into the town. My husband will tell the story of how his grandparents considered putting their farm savings into a trip around the world or alternately building a new retirement house in the town. They chose to build. That option has been a long-lasting investment. The house in the town has been a home, not only for the grandparents for the rest of their lives but for many families and friends since then. It has proven to be a very comfortable home for us too. If the grandparents had spent their money on a world trip, the investment would have finished with the trip. The Bible talks about investing in things that last.

We had a choice to make when we retired from farming. We could have sold the farm and lived quite comfortably for the rest of our lives but instead, we passed the farm over to our son and his family. They are the fourth generation to farm that property. We have an ongoing investment- the pleasure of visiting our farm regularly, watching our grandchildren ride their bikes and feed pet lambs, seeing our son and daughter-in-law make improvements, planting more trees and enjoying the same lifestyle we enjoyed.

Some people have sold their businesses and invested their time and money into serving their community. Other people have only managed from day to day; their circumstances have prohibited them from leaving anything of monetary value to their family or their community. While investing a life's savings can be a lasting investment, our relationships and contributions socially and spiritually can also be an ongoing investment.

"Lord God, help us to understand where and what you want us to invest our time and energy into this year. We want our contribution to have eternal value. Thank you for the good decisions that others have made, which have benefited us. Thank you, Jesus."

1 Timothy 6:17-19
Command those who are rich in this present world not to be arrogant nor to put their hope in wealth, which is so uncertain, but to put their hope in God, who richly provides us with everything for our enjoyment. Command them to do good, to be rich in good deeds, and to be generous and willing to share. In this way they will lay up treasure for themselves as a firm foundation for the coming age, so that they may take hold of the life that is truly life.

'Just a Reminder-Each Day'

Love is a Safe Word

The whole concept of love, being loved, loving someone or something, feeling loved, showing love and God is love, conjures up a sense of safety. It could be compared to sitting on a comfy lounge chair with a cuppa. No expectations! All is well! Life is good!

I have the wonderful benefit of loving and being loved by my husband. I admit to having similar feelings when I look at our children and grandchildren and marvel at the people they are growing into.

Love is often used in reference to God and Jesus. The Bible verse John 3: 16 *For God so loved the world that he gave his one and only son, that whoever believes in him shall not perish but have eternal life,* is probably the most well-known verse in the Bible because it strives to explain how much love God has for the world. For all of us.

We know the word 'love' plays an integral part in this verse, but often, we pass over it and get to the part about being saved. If we could fully understand the concept of love, the incredible sacrifice of allowing one's own child to die for a cause, we would probably find believing a bit easier. This is perfect love. It is so different to human love. Ours is temporary, fallible, sometimes fake, often conditional and always less than perfect.

We cannot measure God's love by comparing it with human love; there is no comparison. To experience and know His love, we need to go straight to God; to trust him to love us, to be vulnerable and to allow his love to shape our lives because his love is a safety net.

"Lord God, I thank you for loving us just as we are. Please show us your perfect and safe love. We want to trust you and allow you to love us the way no person can. Help us to see your love in a practical form, not just in feelings. Thank you, Jesus."

1 Corinthians 13: 4-8
Love is patient, love is kind. It does not envy, it does not boast, it is not proud. It is not rude it is not self-seeking; it is not easily angered; it keeps no record of wrongs. Love does not delight in evil but rejoices with the truth. It always protects, always trusts, always hopes, always perseveres. Love never fails.

'Just a Reminder-Each Day'

April 28
Give Freely

At a time when my mother and I needed help, some very close friends came to our aid. A quick follow-up phone call from our friends reassured us of their support. I could tell my mother was comforted by this news. Over several months, our friends did a lot to help us until, finally, we were settled in our new home. The big move for us took a little adjusting but, eventually, we got on our feet.

We had no specific intentions of repaying our friends; it just happened naturally. Their children were growing in their keenness to be involved in the Pony Club, in which my mother held the position of the head instructor. Mum not only helped our friends' children with their horse-riding skills at the Pony Club but also went to their home when extra help was needed.

I don't believe people should feel they have to return a favour because some people can't and, usually, favours are done without expecting anything in return.

When Jesus suggested to his followers to give because the amount they gave would be given back to them, they may have found it hard to believe or trust that it would work that way. He was introducing a different attitude, not just in giving but in receiving. He was telling them they would get back much more than they expected. We can't outgive God. He is generous and wants us to consider being generous, also.

The rewards we get when we give generously are most likely satisfaction, fulfilment and insight into the way the Holy Spirit works in us for the benefit of others. That can be very exciting.

Lord God, your suggestion that we should give confidently can be a bit different to what we are used to. Please help us trust that if you say we will receive back as much as we have given, it will be. "Thank you, Jesus."

Luke 6: 38
(Jesus said) Give, and it will be given to you. A good measure, pressed down, shaken together, and running over, will be poured into your lap. For with the measure you use, it will be measured to you.

'Just a Reminder-Each Day'

April 29
A Community of People

A friend with whom we shared church and local community events was losing her battle with cancer. At the end of one of our church services the congregation were acutely aware of our friend's situation. She was too sick to attend church anymore. Everyone just sat quietly. There was such a massive sense of God's presence that no one seemed to move; a defining moment. Did we have to let her go and be with the Lord or were we called to pray again for her healing because it felt like the compassion and power of God were right there with us? The air was holy and silent, people were held in a timeless moment. Then gradually, we all stood up and moved out. The moment was gone. I am sure none of us knew what to do with that moment when God seemed to be in our midst. If someone had been confident enough to lead us into prayer for our friend's healing, would we have seen a miracle? Our small church community had been praying as best we could but, finally, our friend died. We were left to accept that which we found ourselves powerless to change and with a grieving family to support and comfort.

Sadly enough, there will always be a community somewhere affected by tragedy and struggling to recover. What helps so much is the relationship between those directly affected and those who have been indirectly affected. Church has lost a lot of its popularity, but when it comes to getting through difficult times, people are often drawn back to it.

The benefits of belonging to a group of people in an uncompetitive environment, are many, where each one cares for the other and all know that God cares for them. Jesus is the perfect mediator. He is the healer and restorer of broken hearts and he offers eternal life, which gives comfort to those who are grieving. Society may benefit if the church was meeting people's needs more effectively.

"Lord God, you don't save us from every tough part of life, but you do stand by us and comfort us, and in due time we find peace. Thank you for being faithful and very present with us in our time of uncertainty. Thank you, Jesus."

Isaiah 43:2
When you pass through the waters, I will be with you; and when you pass through the rivers, they will not sweep over you. When you walk through the fire, you will not be burned.

'Just a Reminder-Each Day'

Life Goes On – So Does Jesus

Australians continue to be dedicated to their summer and winter sports. Families line the courts and ovals to support the stars of the future. Parents, grandparents, friends and coaches are invested in the weekend of sport. The atmosphere is competitive but usually supportive. It is alive with anticipation.

After Jesus died and had ascended into heaven, his disciples were unsure what their future would be. Some were confident that Jesus would return soon, so there was little reason to do anything but wait. Others powered on to share their faith with a determination to tell the whole world about Jesus the Saviour. They learnt so much more about Jesus, God the Father and his Spirit as they lived out their faith. The stories we read in the book of Acts testify to the exciting and often very dangerous lives the disciples led.

Jesus hasn't returned, but his Spirit is with us in our weekend of sport and friendships and all our other activities. We may find ourselves praying for our team to win or for an umpire to be fair. God's kingdom comes where we live, pray, give encouragement and even when we witness to the footy fan standing beside us.

"Lord God, please help us see you in sports, hobbies, work, social life, families and in all situations. Open our eyes to be conscience of your Holy Spirit even in the most unlikely circumstances of our lives. Thank you, Jesus."

Acts 1: 3,8

After his suffering, he showed himself to these men and gave many convincing proofs that he was alive. He appeared to them over a period of forty days and spoke about the kingdom of God. Verse 8 (Jesus said) "But you will receive power when the Holy Spirit comes on you; and you will be my witnesses in Jerusalem, and in all Judea and Samaria and to the ends of the earth."

‘Just a Reminder-Each Day’

On Bare Ground

On a recent trip to Eyre Peninsula, it was sobering to see many paddocks, large paddocks, as bare as the beach. Not a blade of grass or stubble on them. But off in the distance was a large tractor hitched to a large air-seeder and a large tip truck ready to load the seed for planting those incredibly bare paddocks. It is a huge stretch of the imagination to believe that seed will germinate, crops will grow and finally be harvested. The reason those farmers are out there planting grain in such hopeless, dry-looking conditions is that they have, in years gone by, experienced the miracle of rain. They have seen crops emerge and grain develop from what was once a dry paddock. It may not have been last year or the year before but it has happened, and the rewards have been great.

We often hesitate to pray for tough situations such as healing, difficult family issues to be resolved, the bringing down of a dictator or an end to wars. We may even wonder if God is listening. If we ask in faith, there is a bigger chance we will get help and consequently experience God in a new light.

Jesus once told his disciples that if they didn't ask, they wouldn't receive! Those Eyre Peninsula farmers, whose land is often dry and bare must take a risk if they want to have a chance of reaping a good crop. Trusting God and asking for help can go hand in hand with planting into dry ground.

There are times in our lives when we need the courage to try some-thing new, take a risk or just keep going at what we are doing, even when the odds seem against us.

"Lord God, please remind us to take everything to you in prayer, to ask and trust you for the outcome. Thank you that you are faithful and always attentive to our needs. Thank you, Jesus."

James 4: 2
You do not have because you do not ask God.

'Just a Reminder-Each Day'

Decision Time

From a parent's perspective, it is a worry when our children, particularly our teens, are faced with temptations. When they are asked to do what they would not normally do, it is a concern, especially when they are asked to do something without having the time or experience to make the right decision. Young people will persuade each other to try new things, take risks, behave inappropriately, and some will bully anyone who doesn't want to be involved.

The Pharisees had brought a woman caught in adultery and reminded Jesus that the law of Moses commanded them to stone her. "Now what do you say?" they asked him. Jesus surprised them when he bent down and started to write on the ground with his fingers. We can presume Jesus was praying to his Heavenly Father for wisdom or just waiting for the situation to calm down. His answer disturbed those accusers so, one by one, they left. Such wisdom in the face of controversy shows us that we can pray for our children, grandchildren and others to have wisdom under pressure.

During a religious school seminar, a group of us, representing different churches, presented Christianity and the subject of euthanasia along with other social justice issues. A student asked me, specifically, what I thought about euthanasia. I was caught off guard because I had not thought through the topic enough. I knew what I believed but did not have a substantial answer. I was disappointed with myself for going to the school so unprepared.

Maybe Jesus was unprepared when he was asked about the woman's fate, but his answer was amazing.

"Lord God, how nice it would be if we could answer all life's questions with your wisdom and truth. Please help us to become more aware of the way you want things done. Thank you, Jesus."

John 8: 7, 10,11
When they kept on questioning him, he straightened up and said to them, "If any of you is without sin, let him be the first to throw a stone at her." Jesus straightened up and asked her, "Woman, where are they? Has no-one condemned you?" "No-one, sir," she said. "Then neither do I condemn you," Jesus declared. "Go now and leave your life of sin."

May 3
Boris

We started to drive out of our farm gateway when I saw what I thought was our neighbour's black cat. I mentioned to my husband that it seemed the cat was a long way from its home, but then I realised it was a pup huddled under a bush. I stepped out of the vehicle and picked up the black, short-haired, very grateful pup. Back in the utility, he wriggled around excitedly in my lap. It was easy to see the little fellow needed food so I offered him a bit of my sandwich, but he couldn't get enough of being touched to consider eating. We cancelled our plan to do some fencing and took the pup home. I called neighbours hoping to find his owners, but no one knew anything about the stray pup. We fed him and met his need for love and security. As the weeks and months went by, no owner was found. My husband did mention that this breed of dog would never make a sheepdog, so he was useless to us. We named him Boris anyway.

I should have been cautious about keeping him because he had the face of a tough bull terrier and the attitude of a blue heeler. When he got old enough to be in the sheep yard, he had to wear a muzzle. He learnt to work the sheep almost as well as a sheepdog. Boris was a people lover but looked more like a vicious guard dog. He spent his whole life with us. We have story after story of what pleasure Boris gave us. Even our teenagers, their friends and visitors loved Boris. He had a bad habit of cutting the boys off when they were riding their motorbikes, so that had to be stopped. He loved swimming in the dam and would do lap after lap. He would follow me when I rode my horse around the paddock, even the horse enjoyed the dog's company. We never did work out why the stray pup ended up at our gateway. What was God thinking? I think God takes pleasure in giving us gifts, like a stray pup, purely to make us happy. It was not as if we needed another dog! There was some adapting to be done, but his company continued to bless us

"Lord God, are there things in our lives that you have given us, just for our pleasure? We praise and thank you for every good thing you have given us throughout our lives. Thank you, Jesus."

Zephaniah 3: 17
The Lord your God is with you, he is mighty to save. He will take great delight in you, he will quiet you with his love, he will rejoice over you with singing.

‘Just a Reminder-Each Day’

May 4
Through the Tough Times

One night when our two primary school-age children were quite uncomfortable with colds, I set them and myself up to sleep in the lounge room. I was prepared to get little sleep, but I knew I could keep our old farmhouse room warm by stoking the open fire all night. Sleeping with the children seemed the best option. What I didn't predict was how much I would accomplish that night. More than being there for the children each time they coughed, sneezed or just needed comforting, God inspired me to write. Between their disturbed sleep, I started compiling lessons for our small country Sunday School.

By the time the sun came up, I had written a full term of lessons with crafts to go with each lesson. God had given me one idea after another. Even the craft was ten new ideas straight from his Spirit. The best part was that when the children needed me, I was fully awake and deep in thought and conversation with the Lord, so it was easier than usual to be kind and willing to pray for them. I realise this would not have worked out so well if I was a single parent needing to go to work the next day. I know how privileged I am as a stay-at-home Mum with a husband who can take over caring for the children while I catch up on sleep.

"Lord God, please help us see you in the tough times, marvel at your greater plan and trust you are at the end of each dark tunnel. Please

surprise us occasionally with special, close encounters with you. Thank you, Jesus."

Romans 8: 35,37
Who shall separate us from the love of Christ? Shall trouble or hardship or persecution or famine or nakedness or danger or sword (or sickness)- No in all these things we are more than conquerors through him who loved us.

'Just a Reminder-Each Day'

Grace Received but Not Reciprocated

Understanding the meaning of Grace is imperative to understanding the true nature of God. The undeserved favour God shows us when he forgives and accepts us without judgment is His grace. Most people appreciate God's grace. We need it! We need to experience that unique offer for us personally because we all know we fail sometimes, and it feels good to be forgiven and loved just as we are. Life can be hard enough, particularly if we don't know that someone cares for us unconditionally.

The ability to offer Grace to others is a whole different scenario. Consider the last time someone offended you, cheated on you, gossiped about you, ignored you or disrespected you; it hurts! We usually want to tell someone, get it off our chest, retaliate, sulk or withdraw. It is probably healthier to share our hurt with someone, but when we continue to complain we are no longer acting with Grace. We have taken the matter into our own hands to right the wrong. Being able to offer Grace means, first, we need to take it to God and tell him how offended we are. While God's comfort is at work in us, we need to deliberately choose to forgive our offender, even if it is almost impossible to do. Forgiveness does not have to have feelings of forgiveness. It just has to be done, spoken to God and left with him. It is easy to feel we must justify our hurts, but true Grace, which God extends to us, is what we need to offer others to stop the hurt from growing any bigger.

"Lord God, you know how hard it is to be gracious when we have been badly treated. Please help us to fully understand how your grace towards us works so we can reciprocate it. Thank you, Jesus."

Hebrews 12: 15
See to it that no-one misses the grace of God and that no bitter root grows up to cause trouble and defile many.

$\diamond$

May 6
Soup

Either you like soup, or you don't. If you like it, you will probably have a favourite soup. It is wonderful on a cold day. My mother used to make pasty slabs. When we returned from a cold and occasionally wet horse-riding time with our Hunt Club, we would finish the day off with hot soup and slices of pasty straight from the oven decorated with tomato sauce. It was yummy!

This pattern of putting ourselves through hardship and rewarding ourselves at the end shows up in so many aspects of our lives. Football and netball players will push through all sorts of cold, wet and windy weather until the game is finished and then they share a meal and drinks with family and fans. Fishermen will stay out in tough weather, waiting for that magic tug on the line, hoping to return home with a rewarding feed of fresh fish. The home gardener will dig the ground, pull the weeds, rake and level the area while swatting flies and dripping sweat, with the expectation of eating a variety of fruits and vegetables in due time.

For some reason, we tend to feel more deserving if we have endured greater hardships. Jesus certainly endured hardship but also knew victory in the end.

"Lord God, we would rather not have hardships but we appreciate the rewards that can follow. Help us to be willing to endure some hardship when necessary and know that you are our strength. Thank you, Jesus."

John 16: 20-22

I tell you the truth you will weep and mourn while the world rejoices. You will grieve but your grief will turn to joy. A woman giving birth to a child has pain because her time has come; but when her baby is born, she forgets the anguish because of her joy that a child is born into the world. So with you: Now is your time of grief, but I will see you again and you will rejoice, and no-one will take away your joy.

'Just a Reminder-Each Day'

May 7
Over and Over Again

It was a quiet, peaceful day until it was interrupted by a bird. I love birds and welcome their songs but, over and over again, it sang exactly the same thing. I hung more clothes on the line and the bird continued the same short song, over and over again. Finally, I had to look to see what kind of bird was singing such a monotonous song. As my eyes searched in the direction of the sound, the song changed. It went from an uneventful tone to some kind of 'get out of my territory' song. Everything had changed.

Then I noticed a fluffed-up dove walking quickly across the car shed roof in the direction of a visiting honey eater bird. The intruder had barely landed when it was quickly and aggressively ushered off the roof. That was the end of bird songs for a while, but it did remind me of the Bible verses that point out the problems with repetitive prayers, walking around in flowing robes and the deceptive behaviour of the teachers of the Law.

Jesus had been called the 'Lamb of God' but, when it came to pointing out injustice, he was quite outspoken. The dove is often referred to as a symbol of the Holy Spirit, of peace, but this one stood up for what it believed!

We, too, may feel led to climb on our roof and drive an unwanted presence away. In the Lord's prayer, Jesus gives a model of prayer that is assertive and humbling.

"Lord God, please help us when we pray, to be sincere, to be courageous as you are but also with respect for others. Thank you, Jesus."

Mark 12: 38-40
As he taught, Jesus said, "Watch out for the teachers of the law. They like to walk around in flowing robes and be greeted in the marketplaces, and have the most important seats in the synagogues and the places of honour at banquets. They devour widows' houses and for a show make lengthy prayers. Such men will be punished most severely."

'Just a Reminder-Each Day'

Searching for Something

The radio announcer responded to the playing of Handel's Messiah, suggesting that it was an uplifting experience. I had to agree, and it seems to be most people's experience. When the choir declares 'King of Kings, Lord of Lords, Almighty God' with such conviction, our heart is drawn into the celebration. Some part of us wants to worship a higher, majestic being. Those who have decided there is a God and declare their belief in him, understand the feeling of worship, even if it only happens occasionally. Most people are searching for something meaningful. The Christian Church is not necessarily meeting the needs of every searcher. In today's society, there is a general acceptance that we can believe in anyone or anything, and this attitude is becoming more popular. But Jesus came as the Son of God – declaring that he and the Father are One. Peter, the disciple, addressed Jesus and said, *"Lord, to whom shall we go? You have the words of eternal life."* John 6: 68

A YouTube clip was circulating a few years ago where a choir gave what looked like an impromptu recital. The singers were seated randomly in an outdoor eating area in a city mall in Europe. Dressed like they were just part of the usual crowd; one by one they stood and sang. Each blended in with the other until about thirty of them were standing. Dotted throughout the crowd, they sang a soul-stirring worship song as if it were unplanned. I'm so glad a friend passed that clip on to me because the element of surprise amongst the rest of the dining people was captivating and the quality of the performance was even more amazing.

"Lord God, it is a mystery why we are emotionally moved by events with a spiritual connection. It is no mystery that you deserve to be worshipped. Help us understand how it is between you and us, between your spirit and our spirit. Thank you, Jesus."

1 Corinthians 8: 6,7
yet for us there is but one God, the Father from whom all things came and for whom we live; and there is but one Lord Jesus Christ through whom all things came and through whom we live. But not everyone knows this.

A Positive Word at the Right Time

A television program ran a series of stories about athletes who were going to compete in the Para Olympics. One story was of an Australian soldier who had been deployed overseas. He had been part of a small group of men trained to scout ahead for mines, but he became a victim after treading on a mine. He lost both his legs. To add to the problem, he said he was also the paramedic in that group of soldiers. so he had to instruct his men on how to stabilise him, ready to be flown out for treatment. He praised the efforts of his men, but he was aware of the defeated atmosphere amongst them. Finding something positive to say as he was about to be loaded on the rescue helicopter, he turned to his comrades and said, "At least I'll be able to go in the Para Olympics now."

Often, we overlook the positive words given to us in the Bible and miss the encouragement we should have felt. God is all about building up, not tearing down, which can be confused with God's desire for right living. He is a God of righteousness. He offers to help us with our failings so that we will live a more honest and God-respecting life. But he is also an encourager of those having a hard time, as seen in many stories featuring Jesus and his healing power. Matthew 8: 5-13 tells the story of a Centurion who approached Jesus, asking him to heal his servant. The Centurion understood the way an army worked.

He knew that when someone in authority gave an order to a lower-ranked person, it would be obeyed. He told Jesus he believed that if Jesus commanded his servant to be well, he would be. Jesus was very impressed with such faith. In response, he spoke healing into the servant without going to him, just as the Centurion believed he could. Positive words spoken by God have power. That same power is available to us, too.

"Lord God, show us how to think and speak positive words. Thank you, Jesus."

Matt 8: 13
Then Jesus said to the centurion, "Go! It will be done just as you believed it would," and his servant was healed at that very hour.

May 10
Competitiveness

A group of people stood around talking. The topic of sport went to the competitiveness of some players. Each person admitted to being surprised at how a humble, quiet person can change so much once on the court, field or oval. Nice people, it was agreed, become aggressive, out to win at any cost and many of them are above average at their game.

There are so many factors that cause people to change. The desire to outdo an opponent, the drive to achieve a goal, the thrill of pushing one's own body to a higher level, the reward of being recognised as good even the best, the determination to win, and the applause, are all it takes for some people. Our society also exalts the player who not only achieves a high standard but does it with respect and self-control.

Often, we don't acknowledge or even know that the Christian teaching, which has come through the generations, has affected how we conduct our lives, even in sport. We take for granted that it is right to treat your opponent respectfully, but we may have missed where that teaching originated.

"Lord God, thank you for reminding us that it is you who has given us the ideal standards that we all admire whether in sport, families, friendships, business or governing. Thank you, Jesus."

For this very reason, make every effort to add to your faith goodness; and to goodness, knowledge; and to knowledge, self-control; and to self-control, perseverance; and to perseverance, godliness; and to godliness, brotherly kindness; and to brotherly kindness, love. For if you possess these qualities in increasing measure, they will keep you from being ineffective and unproductive in your knowledge of our Lord Jesus Christ.

'Just a Reminder-Each Day'

✧

May 11
Understanding

Being shown something we don't understand is a typical childhood experience. There were plenty of things I didn't understand during my childhood. My way of coping was to find another way of getting around what I did not understand. Sometimes I just accepted the fact that I had failed to understand.

Later, in my adult life, I was keen to help my husband with the farm bookwork. He had always managed well without my help, but the introduction of the GST, Bas statements and computers added to his workload. I thought I could take over, but it was a weird and very distressing experience each time I found I could not get my head around some farm concepts. It was as if I was trying to push a train up a hill. My brain would not budge on specific problems no matter how patiently my husband tried to explain them.

One good thing that came out of those humiliating times was the realisation that I could help others with greater learning difficulties than myself. I had patience, and I had become good at finding other ways of tackling problems.

I still wish I had a better understanding of the things that defeat me, but I have a sense of God's care for me just as I am. Instead of being embarrassed by my inadequacies, I have come to appreciate the people God has put around me who do what I cannot do. I know that my enthusiasm for reading and studying the Bible has been good for me intellectually and spiritually.

"Lord God, it is not fair! You know everything, and I know so little but thank you for giving me the ability to do some things well. Thank you for those people around me who can do even more. Thank you, Jesus."

Psalm 119: 130
The unfolding of your words gives light, it gives understanding to the simple.

'Just a Reminder-Each Day'

Say it with Respect

I paraded out into the lounge room in my new dress and said, "What do you think? How does this one look?" My husband quickly put down his book and gave me his full attention. "It looks nice, but I think I like the first one best," he advised. There are some things we expect of each other in a marriage, and asking our husbands to be as enthusiastic about what we choose to wear for a special occasion is one of those.

Of course, it may not be his favourite thing to do – but we appreciate their opinion as they do ours, occasionally. In all of life, we can benefit from giving each other advice but it needs to be done with love and respect. If we skip the 'love and respect' part, we must live with the consequences.

In the same way, we need to have love and respect for others and want the best for them, particularly when giving them advice. The opportunity to provide advice may come up in group conversations, at a family dinner, at Bible study, in the supermarket, out in the paddock, at a sporting event or in any situation where people share their opinions.

Jesus gave us many perfect examples of how to give wise advice. We might be expecting too much to have the perfect wisdom of God at our disposal but wanting the best for others and praying first is a good start to getting it right.

"Lord God! How can I get it right when it is so easy to open my mouth and put my foot right in it? I look to you to give me the wisdom to say the right thing at the right time. Thank you, Jesus."

Colossians 4: 6
Let your conversation be always full of grace, seasoned with salt, so that you may know how to answer everyone.

✧

May 13

Enough is Enough

I can now say that enough is enough! The apostle Paul said, *"I have learnt the secret of being content."* It is so good for our mental health to recognise when enough is enough and we have all we need. I had envisioned what we could do outside the kitchen window of our house in the town.

Moving into the town to live was a huge time of adjustment. The view from our farm kitchen window, and every other window, in the house was of acres and acres of farmland and all we had invested into our married life. Trees we had planted, sheds, sheepyards and stables all added to the pleasure.

From our house kitchen window in the town, we could only see our neighbour's bedroom window. I guess people who grew up in a town would not understand how incredibly strange this was for us. Gradually we set up a pleasant distraction for our eyes. Archways, plants and shade cloth all helped to change the view. I kept adding more plants and then a bird bath until, one day, I realised enough was enough! Birds came for the water, ivy started to creep over the arch and plants flowered with eye-catching colour. We had made a change that worked for us and it was time to get on with other things.

This change to living in a town came after forty-seven years on our farm. With God's help, we were able to find some peace in the new arrangement. Unlike the apostle Paul, we have not suffered persecution, imprisonment or faced death. His experiences can teach us to know when enough is enough.

"Lord God, please help me when I struggle to know when enough is enough. Thank you for the courage of Paul, who faced more than I can imagine and yet he knew you were with him and that was enough for him. Thank you, Jesus."

Philippians 4: 12
I know what it is to be in need, and I know what it is to have plenty. I have learnt the secret of being content in every and any situation, whether well fed or hungry, whether living in plenty or in want.

'Just a Reminder-Each Day'

Don't Bother God

Society tends to understand God, based on performance. We choose NOT to bother God because we doubt he will meet our needs; we even doubt he cares for us personally and we doubt he CAN make a difference. We doubt that he is doing something in the world anyway, and we doubt his performance will be any better than the other powers we turn to, like doctors, governments and lawyers. We choose NOT to bother God because we are concerned that he may ask us to change, give up something or live differently. Getting too close to God makes us wary that we may lose our identity and personal freedoms. We are hesitant to gain an understanding of God by reading books, searching modern media or asking a friend about what God has to offer.

We find it easy to judge each other based on performance, good or bad. We judge people we don't know without first getting to know them. Australians have been known as people who give others a fair go. But do we give God a fair go? If we haven't seen a miracle or seen something big that we can attribute to God, then we just leave him alone. We happily leave Christianity, the church, seeking Jesus and the pursuit of truth to others. We don't want to bother God.

God is not bothered by us. On the contrary, he cares and accepts us as we are. He wants us to engage with him, take the risk and find out for ourselves if he can be depended on. Yes, we can bother God for our own sake, and he can take it!

"Lord God, I am sorry that I often want to see you do big things before I am willing to trust you. Open my eyes to see all the good things you are doing. Please help me to know that you are worth bothering and how much more I will gain if I go to you with my needs. Thank you, Jesus."

Isaiah 65: 24
Before they call, I will answer; while they are still speaking, I will hear.

'Just a Reminder-Each Day'

Kittens in a Tyre

A newspaper article reported on a litter of kittens discovered inside a tyre. The tyre was part of a load of other tyres going to a disposal sight. The kittens were found in time and instead of being euthanised, they were rescued, fed, named and all their medical needs met, ready for rehoming.

Why do we rescue some and not others? Why do we put a higher value on one life than another? We cull feral cats in National Parks but rescue orphan kittens. Some situations draw on our emotions more than others. We like to save the innocent.

Jesus' death and resurrection rescued us from eternal doom. God is the ultimate rescuer. A taxi driver, in a country where people were desperately fleeing for their lives, rescued an abandoned baby. He took the little one home and cared for it until a family member could be found. On handing the child over to its family, months later, the taxi driver broke down and cried. Clearly, he had not only rescued the baby but cared for it with love.

"Lord God, we honour you as the one who has rescued us for eternity. Thank you for all the other times you rescue us. Please help us to see if we have a role to play in rescuing others. Thank you, Jesus."

Psalm 106: 4,5
Remember me, O Lord, when you show favour to your people, come to my aid when you save them, that I may enjoy the prosperity of your chosen ones, that I may share in the joy of your nation and join your inheritance in giving praise.

'Just a Reminder-Each Day'

Roosters

Roosters tend to have a bad name. They get themselves into trouble and lose favour with people. Some roosters have been known to chase children out of the chook yard while others wake people too early in the morning. In the film Babe, the rooster is the 'bad guy'.

At one stage, when we were staying at our daughter's home, sleeping in their caravan, they had a bantam rooster that delighted in waking us before dawn! Bad rooster! In the story of Jesus, Judas becomes the 'bad guy'. Jesus permits Judas to betray him when he says, "Do what you have to do." Jesus was on a mission and the final part of that was to face his crucifixion.

The 'bad guy' in a story helps us to identify the 'good guy', to take his side, to focus on the good and to shun the bad. In the story of life, God is the good guy. More people are drawn to God than are willing to admit. Some people choose not to acknowledge their affiliation with the church or faith in God on a census form. Still, the human heart longs to be comfortable with God. Secretly, we want God to be our 'good guy', to win our battles for us and to be the hero in our own story.

Two men, Ian McCormack and Jim Woodford, one a New Zealander and the other an American, in their testimonies of being in heaven (their near-death experiences), speak of seeing the bad guy, Satan, on the way to meet the good guy, Jesus. Both men are emotionally moved as they remember how real Satan and hell were, but the most encouraging part is their wonder of being in the presence of God, a feeling they can barely describe because of its out-of-this-world goodness.

"Lord God, please help us to be sure of your goodwill for us. Help us to identify with you as our God and Saviour. Thank you, Jesus."

Psalm 24: 8,10
Who is this King of Glory? The Lord strong and mighty, the Lord mighty in battle.
   Who is he, this King of Glory? The Lord Almighty – he is the King of Glory.

✦

May 17

Trying too Hard

Polocrosse Tournaments were fun. Travelling away from home with our horses and friends, summing up the competition and anticipating the social life was a highlight of the season.

At one tournament, we played the usual round of games on Saturday and at the end of the day, we dined with teammates and many other opposing riders. These tournaments were known for their friendly rivalry. Our relationship with the opposition was almost as good as that with our team members. We enjoyed getting together with familiar faces and making new friends. The Sunday was tradition-ally finals day. The desire to be as fresh and capable of playing as on the first day was always a challenge. The Saturday night partying often took its toll on those who partied too hard.

Our horses were stabled at the show grounds with most of the other horses in the tournament. The friendly conversation around morning feed-up time, exchanging horse stories and assessing each other's level of fitness, was common. My mother, who always played a strong game of polocrosse, was going to take her horse out for a warm-up before giving him his breakfast. A short ride around the grounds was her plan. Not wanting anyone to think she was not fit for the day, she decided to ride bareback (with no saddle). She leapt so high onto her horse that she went straight over the other side. Laughter broke out around the stables as Mum tried again, but this time she didn't try so hard!

Following the life of the apostle Paul, we often read where he tried very hard to convince his listeners that Jesus was the way to be saved.

"Lord God, thank you for the people who try hard to help us and others. Please reward them for their efforts. Thank you, Jesus."

1 Corinthians 10: 31,32,33
So whether you eat or drink or whatever you do, do it all for the glory of God. Do not cause anyone to stumble, whether Jews, Greeks or the church of God - even as I try to please everybody in every way. For I am not seeking my own good but the good of many, so that they may be saved.

May 18

Getting Lost

Asking for directions can be embarrassing but so can asking God for something. We think we should know where we are going. It is not fun getting lost, let alone admitting to it. It points out our weaknesses. We don't get lost in our home area and we are more than happy to direct others around our town and district, so why are we so tentative about getting directions when we need them?

In the early days of using a computer, I was very embarrassed to ask for help, and I needed it often. I knew if I asked for help I might not understand the answer. Click here, double-click there, open this window, drag that, and by then I'm lost!

No matter how good our technology is, we can still get lost. The biggest obstacle isn't being lost, but who to turn to, to get un-lost! Approaching God for help is like admitting we are lost in a place we should know well. If people are so happy to give us directions and our young family members love to sort out our computer and phone problems for us, then it is quite possible that God is even happier to give us all the information and guidance we want. The Bible says many times that God is compassionate and wants to help us.

"Lord God, please help us to take our concerns to you, to ask for help without feeling a fool. We want to see your power and experience your guidance. Thank you, Jesus."

'Just a Reminder-Each Day'

Terms and Conditions

'**D**o you accept the following terms and conditions?' I can't believe how many times that question appears. It doesn't seem long ago that the only time we saw it was when purchasing something large or in business dealings, but nowadays, it turns up frequently on computers and phones. Young people starting jobs, even volunteers are faced with pages of terms and conditions. The extensive fine print is designed to protect the company/employer from litigation. There is less trust in our society and taking responsibility for our mistakes without expecting someone else to pay, is declining.

Christianity should be free from all terms and conditions because the Bible tells us that salvation is a free gift from God. But we tend to put terms and conditions on people; possibly, we don't trust the Holy Spirit to guide new believers or we can't entirely accept that salvation should be totally free for everyone. Being kind, being generous, trying to be a better person, attending church regularly and working hard to grow your faith are all man-made conditions.

In the Old Testament, we find the Jewish people having many rules to live by, striving to be right with their God. In the New Testament, there is a huge shift when the teaching of Jesus shakes up their preconceived ideas. Some gladly accepted the offer of salvation by faith in Jesus with NO terms and conditions.

From the disciples, right throughout history, we see the effects of this gift of salvation on humanity. Some people who have accepted Jesus as Lord, have impacted thousands while others have impacted tens of thousands. St Augustine, John Wesley, Smith Wigglesworth, Billy Graham, Reinhard Bonnke and so many other missionaries, evangelists and untold witnesses have shared their faith, with no terms and conditions. They saw the world change, sometimes, one person at a time.

"Lord God, thank you for your gift of salvation which transforms us from the inside out. Please help us to share our story with no terms and conditions. Thank you, Jesus."

Ephesians 2: 8,9
For it is by grace you have been saved, through faith – and this not from yourselves, it is the gift of God – not by works, so that no-one can boast.

May 20
Overjoyed

'Hello, friend!' I could almost hear our dog say from her position in the back of our Patrol. She wagged her tail and wriggled her body so hard that I felt the car rock against the curb where we were parked. I was not surprised to see a familiar face approaching the car with her hand outstretched to pat our dog. Gretel, our Coolie dog, had noticed her friend coming along the street and was overjoyed to see her. Our friend cupped the dog's face in her hands, telling her what a beautiful dog she was. Gretel had stretched her head out from her back window as far as she could, not wanting to miss out on being patted.

Our friendship with the lady from the agricultural store in our small country town had grown over the years. We shared animal stories, laughed and lamented together. Each time I bought a bag of dry dog or cat food from her she sack trucked the bags to our car and made a big fuss over Gretel who waited patiently for the attention.

The whole event reminded me that Christian teaching should make us feel good about God. We misrepresent God if our witnessing or teaching leaves the listener feeling accused or just not good enough. God doesn't tell us to try harder. On the contrary, God complements us and builds us up. It is the devil who condemns, accuses, points out our faults and leaves us feeling guilty. Understanding that we are loved and accepted by God, just like our dog is so sure this lady loves her, is good for our whole outlook on life.

"Lord God, thank you for showing us your love, for the compliments and encouragement we get from reading your word and understanding your grace. Thank you, Jesus."

1 Chronicles 16: 23, 34
Sing to the Lord all the earth; proclaim his salvation day after day. Give thanks to the Lord, for he is good; his love endures for ever.

'Just a Reminder-Each Day'

✦

May 21

Sit Where You Are Comfortable

If you have ever had the pleasure of choosing a pup from a litter, you will also know it can be difficult. The lady selling her Coolie pups let the seven of them out of their yard and put a dish of food out for them. They waddled around, their short legs barely getting their big tummies off the ground. The lady went on to say there were six males and one female. One pup seemed more interested in sitting on Phil's boot than eating with her brothers. I picked up a gentle-looking male pup, having made my choice, but the female pup, still scrambling over Phil's boots, had won his heart. Gretel became ours and as she matured, we found that whenever she wanted to be close to us, she would sit on our feet. We noticed she wasn't fussy when she took up the sitting position on a friend's boot one day.

I sat down on the bank of our dam and took in all the beauty, the reflection on the water, the carpet of green grass and the serenity of our farm. Gretel, now five years old, planted herself so close to me she was almost sitting in my lap. I was amused to think she had not changed her ways, always looking for the seat of the highest importance.

When Jesus noticed some guests of a prominent Pharisee selecting the most honourable seats at the table, he told his listeners a parable. It was a warning to people to act humbly and not to elevate themselves to a higher position. (Luke 14: 7-11)

In our culture, we usually sit where we are comfortable. Sometimes, like at weddings, we are shown where to sit.

A mother asked Jesus if one of her sons could sit at his right hand and the other at his left. She asked for her sons to have the highest position available when Jesus reigned. (Matthew 20: 23)

"Lord God, thank you for giving us a place of honour that we didn't earn or deserve. Thank you for accepting us as we are. Thank you, Jesus."

Ephesians 2: 6,7
And God raised us up with Christ and seated us with him in the heavenly realms in Christ Jesus, in order that in the coming ages he might show the incomparable riches of his grace, expressed in his kindness to us in Christ Jesus.

'Just a Reminder-Each Day'

✦

May 22
Dust Storms

Dust storms often precede rain which is probably their only redeeming feature. I have enjoyed my life as a farmer's wife but some weather events can make life hard. One year when the opening rains were slow to arrive and we were hand-feeding our sheep each day, a wind blew up with such strength that the dry soil lifted, filling the air with brown grit and causing low visibility. With my utility loaded with bags of grain, I drove around the paddock, hoping the sheep would find me as I couldn't see them in the dust. Eventually, I heard bleating as hungry sheep milled around me. I set the ute going in first gear and ran and hopped on the back. I poured the grain out in a long line on the ground. The dust blew relentlessly into my eyes and mouth while the sheep grabbed mouthfuls of welcome grain.

Clutching an armful of empty bags so they wouldn't fly across the paddock, I jumped off the back and ran to the driver's side door. The wind pushed against me, almost sweeping me off my feet, making the door difficult to pull open. Taking another quick step, I pushed off harder with my right foot, hoping that would land me in the slow-moving ute, but my knee gave out. Desperate to get in the ute rather than have it continue across the paddock without me, I hopped on my left leg and threw myself onto the seat. So relieved to be in the vehicle, with the huge empty bags tangled around me, I sat while the pain of my injured knee took over. My husband was also working in the dust storm trying to fix the air-seeder bar. I drove up beside him and

called out, "I've hurt my knee, I'll be home, the sheep are finished."
With my left leg operating the clutch and accelerator, I managed to
drive to the house.

Slumping down into a soft lounge chair with my knee elevated,
I wished someone was home to get me a comforting coffee and some
pain relief. I survived! Some of life's hard times help us to appreciate
the good times. Whatever work we do, we can honour God with our
good intentions.

*"Lord God, help us appreciate our work and honour you in all our
striving. Thank you, Jesus."*

1 Corinthians 15: 58
*Therefore, my dear brothers, stand firm. Let nothing move you. Always
give yourselves fully to the work of the Lord, because you know that
your labour in the Lord is not in vain.*

'Just a Reminder-Each Day'

May 23
They will Know Us

My tall, slim girlfriend bent down, tucked the tabs of her well-polished brown elastic-sided boots under her straight-leg jeans, laughed and walked on. It was true, we did have an unwritten dress code that defined us. We wanted to be seen as horse-riding country women. My girlfriend grew up in the suburbs and constantly broke that mould to be the person she always wanted to be.

Young people choose to be identified by a symbolic dress code, which is even more obvious in this modern age. Body piercing, tattoos, coloured hair, odd hair lengths, rips in jeans and baggy clothes say it all. Young people, today, tend to group together just like young people did decades ago.

Jesus encouraged his disciples to group together to represent him by the way they treated each other. We may mistake the 'love one another' mentioned here to be affection, arms around each other type of love, but I'm sure Jesus was referring to the 'tough' love that requires forgiving, bearing with each other's differences and working together for the one common cause. The disciples had a new life to lead and it would have its challenges and tough times as they promoted Jesus as Lord and Saviour. The revolutionary effect of knowing the Saviour and his love for them would enable them to love one another beyond the usual comradeship of men.

They would embark on a journey of being witnesses to tell the world a new way of knowing God.

"Lord God, please help us to be your people and representatives by loving one another as you have loved us. Thank you, Jesus."

John 13: 35
By this all men will know you are my disciples if you have love one for the another.

‘Just a Reminder-Each Day’

Bridging the Gap

It can be hard going in relationships where uncomfortable gaps exist, where we disagree rather than agree or we don't have enough in common. This is especially so if we are in the same circle of friends, family or clubs. Awkward relationships can lead to a sense of hopelessness.

Even when we work hard to make these relationships succeed, there can be little or no improvement. With the Holy Spirit of God as our mediator, the One who bridges the gap between God and us,

Friendship

we find he can do the same for our human relationships. When both parties want the same outcome, the Holy Spirit is free to do good things. It is essential that we don't give up on relationships but rather pray for a better result. The devil would be pleased if we gave up and declared any uncomfortable friendship unrepairable.

Asking God to make others in our group happy, rather than wait for them to change, may be a good way of seeing how amazing the work of the Holy Spirit is.

God's way for us is usually to persevere, expect things to get better and keep asking for his help.

"Lord God, thank you for all the relationships in our lives that are positive and enjoyable. Please help us with the ones where we don't connect well enough. Thank you, Jesus."

1 Peter 3: 8
Finally, all of you, live in harmony with one another; be sympathetic, love as brothers, be compassionate and humble.

May 25

Grey to Green

Sometimes I am embarrassed if we have visitors from interstate during our Summer or Autumn seasons. We live in South Australia, the driest state in a dry continent. After the golden heads of the crop have been harvested, the farming landscape generally takes on a neutral appearance, cream, fawn, grey and colourless. Except for the trees and parks around the towns and cities and the plants in our gardens, there is a real lack of green. This can go on for months but when rain does come, the pastures germinate and the planted crops appear. The scene changes! Green is my favourite colour! What a difference it makes as the whole landscape turns green. It's like fresh air, a surprise, a parcel in the post, the arrival of a baby or an unexpected visit from someone special.

Sometimes God gives us a lift, unexpected, undeserved, even unpredicted. We find our spirit is refreshed, like the grey, lifeless countryside when it turns green. You feel good about life. Maybe at that point, someone is praying for us and God is responding.

"Lord God, please help us recognise when it is you giving us that inward lift we need when we least expect it. Please help us to respond to you in gratitude. Thank you for all the life changes that give us renewed hope and the promise of something good still to come. Please reward the people who pray for us. Thank you, Jesus."

Psalm 126: 5,6
Those who sow in tears will reap with songs of joy. He who goes out weeping, carrying seed to sow, will return with songs of joy, carrying sheaves with him.

May 26
Girl's Bible Study

Starting the day with a group of like-minded friends worked well for us. We looked forward to our 2-3 hours on a Thursday morning. Meeting in each other's homes after our children were set for a day at school, we explored the Bible and prayed together. Our weekly event was either focused on a Bible commentary, a women's study guide or just random searching for interesting verses. Our talks were stimulating and sometimes heart-wrenching as we shared personal aspects of our lives. We experimented in prayer, especially in laying hands on each other and expecting God to do big things.

Gradually we came to understand how to use God's Spiritual gifts. Nothing was quite as exciting or taxing as our time together. We cried, laughed, forgave and sometimes got frustrated. There was always so much to learn. We found we could trust each other, bear with each other and, above all else, experience God. The deeper our understanding, the more we wanted. We made plenty of mistakes but all through that we were aware of God's encouragement to keep pushing on. I found some of my most profitable and faith-growing experiences in these gatherings. I am very grateful to the young women with whom I shared those important study mornings.

On one occasion, one of the girls started praying for another and was eager to tell her the Bible reading God had impressed on her the night before. Feeling disappointed, as she struggled to remember it, the thought came to me, Jeremiah 33:3, but I dismissed it. Those numbers were too unlikely, so I said nothing. Days later, I discovered it was exactly as the Lord had told me. It shocked me that God had chosen to speak directly to me, but it also put me on track for future times when God would speak to me.

"Lord God, thank you for the huge encouragement we receive from sharing with friends we can trust. Thank you for your patience in teaching us your ways. Thank you, Jesus."

Jeremiah 33: 3
Call to me and I will answer you and tell you great unsearchable things you do not know.

May 27

Do it Your Way

Australia has been accused of being behind the rest of the world and I guess, in many ways, that is true but catching up hasn't always been good. In the equestrian world, Australia did have some catching up to do. Our horse-riding style was mainly old English, with feet pushed forward onto the horse's shoulders and our upper bodies leaning back.

When European ways were first introduced, we were slow to change, until we were convinced that feet shoved forward and leaning back only served to put riders and horses off balance. Old photos of riders going over jumps and leaning back are a great reminder of where we have come from. Jockeys, show jumpers, dressage riders and stockmen have chosen the better way now and have developed a style that puts the rider's weight where the horse is best able to carry it. The results are far better. What the Australian riders didn't have to change was their experience of riding rough. The Olympic games results for the Three-Day Event competition show Australia has done very well.

It is wise to do something another way if it proves to be the best way. So often 'The Way' as the new Christians in the Bible were labelled, proved too different from the religion they were used to. Many turned their backs and walked away.

In Acts, we get a glimpse of Paul presenting his case to Felix the governor. He included the words Jesus spoke to him on the road to Damascus.

"Lord God, this new way has liberated New Testament people. Please help us to fully grasp how much we have gained. Thank you, Jesus."

Acts 24: 14, 26: 18.
However, I admit that I worship the God of our fathers as a follower of The Way,
*   'I am sending you to them to open their eyes and turn them from darkness to light, and from the power of Satan to God, so that they may receive forgiveness of sins and a place among those who are sanctified by faith in me.'*

'Just a Reminder-Each Day'

May 28
Bright Wheelbarrow

I was mildly amused when I looked around the yard noting how many things were painted a robust bright aqua colour, not only the wheelbarrow but many large and small pots. In some places, the colour looks impressive placed against a contrasting dark green fence. I had picked up what I thought was a bargain, a tin of hardy exterior paint that someone had decided they did not want. When I started painting, I realised why! It was an outstanding colour but wanting to be appreciative of my bargain, I painted many things!

I have come to love the bright aqua bits and pieces around the garden. They stand out and give me pleasure. It can be like having new people move into the area, especially in small country towns. Some people come with a lot to offer, some come because they need a new address and others may come looking for a stable community. Our place, where we live, work and play, may or may not be the best place where we can achieve and find happiness but ultimately, it is God's presence with us that enables us to do something valuable.

It is not our choice initially where we grow up. Some people move around so much that they don't relate to any place as 'where they came from', while others hardly move at all. Farming families are quite likely to stay in the same district all their lives but other professions are likely to be transferred quite a few times in their working life. We don't have to live in certain places to live credible lives. The main thing is to feel good about our position in the big garden.

We can be a brightly coloured wheelbarrow parked by a green fence, catching everyone's attention or an ordinary pot hidden under many green plants, unseen but still being the home of a showy plant. Find God, find life!

"Lord God, please help us to recognise the value of where you have positioned us. Help us to reflect your goodness and to see what your ongoing plan is for us. Thank you, Jesus."

James 2: 5
Listen, my dear brothers: Has not God chosen those who are poor in the eyes of the world to be rich in faith and to inherit the kingdom he promised those who love him?

Run Forrest Run

The movie Forrest Gump won many awards. The story elevated an intellectually slow man to hero status. The well-written film draws the audience into being on the side of Forrest, a boy who is bullied but liberated by a girl who believes in him. Forrest finds that he can run fast and run for a long time. Later in the film as a soldier, this talent leads him to become a decorated war hero. Forrest rescues many fellow soldiers during a bloody battle where his friends are injured.

Forrest used his ability by running into the firing area and bringing wounded men, one by one, out into a safe area. Intellectually, Forrest was not able to evaluate the risk of the rescue mission. Instead, he just went and did what seemed a natural thing to do.

Christianity can look like an institution for comfortable living people with no risk attached to it. Jesus was a great risk-taker and role model for all of us. There is a huge risk in following Jesus into the war zone if we really want the excitement. Even the first step we took when we believed in Jesus, the Messiah who could save us for eternity, was a life-changing event.

Witnessing, locally or beyond, teaching about Jesus, writing about faith in a living God, telling people our story of conversion, praying for healing, delivering people from demons, fighting for justice and working in places where Christianity is unpopular, can all be a considerable risk.

Preceding this Bible reading, Paul tells the Corinthians that he gets beside people in a way they will understand. He does that to win people to Jesus.

"Lord God, help us run the race you have mapped out for us confidently. Please help us to take risks where the prize has eternal value. Thank you, Jesus."

1 Corinthians 9: 24,25
Do you not know that in a race all the runners run, but only one gets the prize? Run in such a way as to get the prize. Everyone who competes in the games goes into strict training. They do it to get a crown that will not last; but we do it to get a crown that will last for ever.

May 30

Think about Such Things

Negative thoughts can lead to bad decisions. What we think affects the way we behave. If we are swayed by other people's opinions, tempted to go with the crowd, attracted only to popular ideas and not giving attention to the Holy Spirit's direction, we can end up anywhere. It's a big ask to be totally focused on the right path when we have so many influences coming at us from all directions. The choices through modern media are endless; some are more harmful than good.

For our own sake, we need to feed on the positive effects of God's word. A small amount of time spent each day on something 'God inspired' can give us good direction for the rest of the day and into the week. If we focus on health problems rather than giving thought to the healing power of Jesus, or we think too much about past failures rather than God's promise to lead us in his ways, we can miss the comfort of his Spirit and the victory we have in Jesus Christ. The Bible is God's word for our benefit; it safeguards against negative advice and the selfish demands of our modern world. We can trust his word to bring confidence and encouragement when we most need it.

"Lord God, thank you for your written word and the insight and empowerment it can give us. Please help us to find time to read it and be built up each day. Thank you, Jesus."

Philippians 4: 8
Finally brothers (sisters) whatever is true, whatever is noble, whatever is right, whatever is pure, whatever is lovely, whatever is admirable - if anything is excellent or praiseworthy - think about such things.

‘Just a Reminder-Each Day’

May 31
Discipline by Love

growled at our dog Gretel for barking. She came back apologetically. I held her and explained that she should be used to the noisy utility and trailer that just passed our back fence. I reminded her that it goes past at least once a week, so she did not need to bark. I went on hanging the clothes on the line but I was very aware that Gretel was staying close, hoping I would not growl at her again.

Many years ago, the first time I heard people talking about God disciplining us, I questioned it. Sure, he wants us to live a good life but I'm a bit like the dog. I cower down and almost hide when I'm corrected. I hate it! It hurts! I believe God is different; his ways are different from ours. I question, then, how does God discipline us without hurting us and driving us away? He is diplomatic and kind while committed to leading us away from wrongdoing.

The Holy Spirit leads us into the truth, so it seems God leads us away from doing wrong by building us up to want to do the right thing. The nudging and guiding we experience is God's Spirit at work within us.

His way is easier to accept compared with external voices that tell us what to do and where to go. Maybe holding the dog was a way of building her up to continue trusting me after I had disciplined her.

"Lord God, thank you for correcting us gently and respectfully. Thank you for revealing the truth, so we know the best way to go. Holy

Hebrews 12: 5,6
My son, do not make light of the Lord's discipline, and do not lose heart when he rebukes you, because the Lord disciplines those he loves.

Holidays to Remember

When our children were primary school age, we drove inter-state to Western Australia to a friend's wedding. There were lots of fun things to do on the way especially exploring the abandoned Eucla outpost telegraph station. Only a few walls were left exposed after years of wind had moved tons of white sand up against the old limestone buildings. There were no roofs left, just the bare walls. In its day, 1877, it was the largest Telegraph Station on the East-West telegraph line and it played an essential role in transmitting between South Australia and Western Australia from 1896 to 1905.

Our children had a wonderful time rolling down the sandhills, only to climb up again and roll faster the next time. My husband has always been good at remembering to photograph such occasions. A photo we have is of our children on one side of the stone wall, which was built up with sand high enough for them to rest their chins on top of the wall. On the other side, the wind had eroded the sand away, exposing the full height of the wall. It looked quite intriguing. Photos help us remember holidays and all sorts of special occasions that may otherwise fade in our memory.

The Israelites were told to remember the goodness of God – the way he brought them out of slavery in Egypt. (Deuteronomy 6: 12). No cameras in those days just stories to pass on! It is so important that we remember the good times, the help we have received and who we can thank.

"Lord God, please help us remember the good things we have experienced and how you have watched out for us and made such advancements possible. Thank you, Jesus."

Psalm 103: 2-5
Praise the Lord O my soul and forget not all his benefits – who forgives all your sins and heals all your diseases, who redeems your life from the pit and crowns you with love and compassion, who satisfies your desires with good things so that your youth is renewed like the eagles.

‘Just a Reminder-Each Day’

June 2

Winter is Here!

Winter marks the beginning of growth. Dormant paddocks come alive as the green shoots emerge and grow into crops. Weeds threaten to take over the garden! Growth is something we take for granted but it is deeply rooted in our world. Our human body grows until it reaches adulthood. God himself is all about growth. He created and he continues to grow his creation. As farmers or home gardeners, we can be diligent in how we plant and fertilise but growth is inherent. Nothing man can take credit for! This is one of the wonders of our world.

The growth of a person, physical, emotional, intellectual and spiritual has God's full attention. We can be deceived into thinking God plants and then forgets, or in the case of people, he sets them up to live and then abandons them.

It is easy to shy away from any involvement with God if we are uncertain about his interest in our lives. Still, if the growth of a plant is any indication as to how committed God is to life, not failure, then surely he is even more committed to our development.

All too often, the term, 'moving forward', is used by politicians and leaders because they know we need something to hope for and grow towards. God's not out of the picture here. He invented growth. His ultimate plan for all people is to know him and trust the plans he has for them. Physical, mental and spiritual growth and achievement are essential for happiness.

"Lord God, help me to reach my full potential. I want to grow in the knowledge of your love and care for me. I want to be aware of your Spirit at work in me so that with you, I can make a decent mark on my patch and be a useful figure in my community. Thank you, Jesus."

Isaiah 58: 11
The Lord will guide you always; he will satisfy your needs in a sun-scorched land and will strengthen your frame. You will be like a well-watered garden, like a spring whose waters never fail.

June 3

In My Weakness

"Thank you, Lord, you're so good to me," I uttered. But I wondered if I would get the rose thorn out of the awkward position in my right hand. I went for the tweezers, but all the time I was wondering how I would direct my left hand to do the job. I doubted the light would be good enough to see what I was doing, even with my glasses on. That was probably the penalty I was paying for working in the garden until sunset. When my wobbly left hand landed the tweezers on either side of the rose thorn and pulled it out, I was extremely grateful and told the Lord so. There is nothing like the pain inflicted by a thorn to keep us preoccupied.

The apostle Paul described a revelation he had, an out-of-the-body experience, which took him to places man had never gone before, let alone returned to talk about. Those experiences totally convinced him about the Lordship of Jesus and probably a lot more truths about God. In the following Bible reading, we don't know what Paul's thorn was, except that he claims it was sent to keep him humble and reliant on God. Paul was once a very powerful man. He proved that it wasn't a weakness to let God empower him. Paul said he had to accept his weakness so Christ's power could rest on him. We can take our weakness to God and ask him to remove it, but like Paul, if we don't get set free, we can let God use us just as we are. His power in our weakness.

"Lord God, I present to you all my weaknesses. Please heal what you will heal and remove what you will remove but, above all, please allow your power to rest on me. Help me to say like Paul, 'When I am weak then I am strong.' Thank you, Jesus."

2 Corinthians 12:7-10
To keep me from becoming conceited because of these surpassingly great revelations, there was given me a thorn in my flesh, a messenger of Satan to torment me. Three times I pleaded with the Lord to take it away from me. But he said to me, 'My grace is sufficient for you, for my power is made perfect in weakness.' Therefore, I will boast all the more about my weaknesses, so that Christ's power may rest on me. That is why, for Christ's sake I delight in weaknesses, in insults, in hardships, in persecutions, in difficulties. For when I am weak then I am strong.

Through a Rainbow

What an enjoyable day it has been today. We hitched the trailer on and left the farm to pick up a load of firewood from the local supplier. The sun was trying to shine through some heavy clouds that had the potential to rain on us. The sight of crops emerging in the paddocks, roadsides greening up and hardly a breeze to sway the trees added to the experience. The muddy puddles on the dirt roads were drying up and easy to negotiate.

Suddenly a rainbow loomed in the distance but this one looked unusually close, closer than I had ever seen before. Closer, closer, "O, it's gone!" I exclaimed to my husband, looking around quickly to see where it had gone. "We must have driven through it!" I added, not wanting any scientific explanation that would spoil the magic. It just felt mystical!

Further along our journey, as if driving through a rainbow was not enough, we noticed a wombat nibbling on the grass on the side of the road. At first glance, it looked like a big lump of dirt but when we backed up to photograph it, there was no sign of the marsupial. We didn't want to scare it, so we headed off to get our wood, rejoicing over the rare sighting.

"Lord God, you have ways of making your presence felt when we least expect it. Thank you, Jesus."

Genesis 9: 12-15

And God said, (to Noah), "This is the sign of the covenant I am making between me and you and every living creature with you, a covenant for all generations to come: I have set my rainbow in the clouds, and it will be the sign of the covenant between me and the earth. Whenever I bring clouds over the earth and the rainbow appears in the clouds, I will remember my covenant between me and you and all living creatures of every kind. Never again will the waters become a flood to destroy all life.

June 5

Programmed for Success

I knelt by the wood fire in our lounge room and frowned at the flickering fire. I get a little irritable if I have failed to set the fire well enough and it goes out. While I watched the feeble flames and wondered if the fire would succeed or fail, I considered the idea that the fire was programmed to burn anyway. Fire will burn if there is dry wood and not too much wind. Fire burns all too well in hot, dry conditions across paddocks, scrubs, forests and towns when we don't want it to.

As the fire gained momentum, I considered all the other things in our world that seemed programmed to do something regularly and successfully. The sun rises and sets, the tide comes in and it goes out, plants flower and trees produce fruit. So much of life reproduces. Rain falls and the sun warms, birds build nests and man builds bridges, but what impresses me and helps me so much is how our bodies are programmed to heal. Physically and mentally, we are programmed to get well. Unfortunately, our program mechanism is not perfect in this imperfect world.

Spiritually, we seem to be programmed to worship. We can direct our worship to film and music stars, war heroes, new ideas, monarchs and all types of religions and charismatic figures. Documentary presenters of the wonders of this world don't necessarily give credit to the creator for the way all creatures seem programmed to live.

According to the Bible, the truth is that God the Father, Son and Spirit can take credit for all life.

"Lord God, thank you for this marvellous world you have given us to enjoy. Please remind us that our body is programmed to heal. When we experience anxiety about our health or someone else's health, please direct us to pray in Jesus' name for healing. Thank you, Jesus."

Nehemiah 9:6
You alone are the Lord. You made the heavens, even the highest heavens, and all their starry host, the earth and all that is on it, the seas and all that is in them. You give life to everything and the multitudes of heaven worship you.

June 6
Worst Jobs

I think the job I disliked the most on the farm was greasing the slasher. The universal joints where the grease nipples hid so cleverly behind a hard rubber cover were almost impossible to find. When you did find them, it was dark and hard to see which way up the nipple was facing and by the time you held back the cover and positioned the grease gun, your hand would be tired and demanding a rest! I'm not sure how God tolerated my attitude as I cursed the job, swore, got very angry and gave him a piece of my mind for not making the job easier. It did help a little to keep my mind focussed on the end result and envision the paddock nicely mowed and looking like a manicured oval.

The number one most hated job around the house must be hanging wet clothes on an outdoor clothesline in the wind. Getting hit in the face by wet towels as you chase a maniac clothesline driven by wind that has travelled ten kilometres, uninterrupted, from the ocean to our farm, isn't fun!

I must conclude that my God is amazing. He is tolerant, patient, forgiving, slow to anger, understanding, faithful and worthy of my appreciation.

"Lord God, thank you for bearing with us in life's trials and not giving up on us. Thank you for equipping us to succeed even when we are sure we won't make it. Thank you, Jesus."

Micah 7: 19
Who is a God like you, who pardons sin and forgives the transgression of the remnant of his inheritance? You do not stay angry for ever but delight to show mercy.

Jonah 4: 2
I knew that you are a gracious and compassionate God, slow to anger and abounding in love.

'Just a Reminder-Each Day'

June 7

Good Luck

It was a slightly apprehensive but friendly situation where a small group of adults awaited their COVID-19 vaccination. They talked about farming and other country-related subjects. "Rob!" called the nurse as one of those waiting stood up and followed her to the vaccination room. "Good luck!" another man called, and everyone laughed.

It reminded me of a Sunday School subject I taught one day. I instructed the young people on the pointlessness of trusting in luck. I told them that we could think that luck is on our side or it can give us success, but in reality, it has no power at all. I told them that if we want success, then we should go to God as he can make changes. A couple of the young men in the class started talking about how this 'not trusting luck' might play out. "Next week before the footy game starts, if I am not going to say to my opponent 'Good Luck', what am I going to say?" It was a good question, a fun conversation and a good point. If we are going to take seriously what we are putting our hope in, luck doesn't hold much weight. The boys threw around a few ideas like "God be with you" and "Have a good game." They all agreed it would at least get people thinking. Not a bad conversation to have with a group of 10, 11 and 12-year-old boys!

As adults, we are living in a society where buying lottery tickets and investing in the stock market are just some ways where we hope to get 'lucky'. We, too, say 'Good Luck' but, seriously, who do we think will make the difference? It takes courage to expose how we actually think.

If we were to say, 'God be with you' or 'God bless you,' it could be embarrassing, but it could also be his opportunity to bless someone.

"Lord God, we know 'luck' has no power but sometimes we need to be reminded that you are the God of all power, the God who wants the best for us. Please help us to get into perspective the importance of acknowledging you even when we go out to play sports. Thank you, Jesus."

Acts 4:31
After they prayed, the place where they were meeting was shaken. And they were all filled with the Holy Spirit and spoke the word of God boldly.

June 8
Newspapers

After attending church with my boyfriend, I was surprised to find he wanted to buy a newspaper. Back at my home, Phil read the paper while my mother and I chatted and got lunch ready. I had a lot to learn about this new boyfriend, his love of reading, his interest in world affairs, religion, politics, local news, social justice and almost any commendable thing you read in a newspaper, especially the comics. It was a big part of his makeup. Decades later, my husband still loves to read the newspaper and share what he has learned with his family and friends.

The arrival of the internet almost destroyed the newspaper industry. Some small country newspapers closed and some down-sized. Gradually, reading the newspaper returned to play an important part in our modern society.

The desire to know more about God, the Bible and the life of Jesus and his followers has drawn people to search out any printed information that may shine some light on the hidden past. We look to authenticate our faith and the history of Christianity. We want to know the truth to be sure of what we believe.

At one time, our Saturday paper included a puzzle that took some solving. I loved it when our grandsons were with us, leaning over the table, all trying to solve the puzzle together.

The disappointing thing about newspapers is the damaging gossip, exaggerated stories, misleading information and the determination to report anything, regardless of whether it is morally right or not. Sensationalising stories at any cost should not be acceptable.

My husband's love of reading often leads him to share inspirational, enlightening articles that exalt God and reveal the truth and influence of Christianity in our world. Intending to show any interested persons, he carries around newspaper articles, books heavily underlined and any other written matter that may inform or lead others in their faith in God. His influence is quiet and consistent, worthy of acclamation.

"Lord God, we take this opportunity to thank you for those who share their faith, inspire us and direct the way we think. Thank you, Jesus."

Psalm 119: 105
Your word is a lamp to my feet, and a light for my path.

'Just a Reminder-Each Day'

June 9

"Come over to My Place"

"Come over to my place" was a request often heard in my primary school years. Leaving the schoolyard of a very small country school, students could be heard inviting someone over to their place to play. These were times when we walked the town visiting friends, well before terrorist attacks in our country or anything else to fear. Children rode bikes from one friend's house to another. Some rode out to farms and farm children rode into the town. Games were created as we went, which may have been building cubby houses in the scrub on the roadside, looking for rabbits around burrows or just walking along the beach collecting shells. There were very few instructions or warnings given by parents as we left the house, except, "Make sure you are home before dark." Our communication was sometimes a 'cooee' across the town or a note passed from one to another for someone else. The telephone was for adult use and usually hung on the wall, too high for children to reach.

Our modern world has unfortunately brought with it many extra fears and stresses. The simple life of the past will probably stay in the past, as we find it very hard to give up any modern-day pleasures, comforts and new inventions.

Jesus travels through time with us, offering us protection and stability. He is there to help us with the things we can't manage independently. Each generation has the chance to walk in the light of the Lord and see things that only he reveals.

"Lord God, thank you for all those special childhood experiences we hang onto and sometimes wish we could return to. Help us to see you and follow you in every stage of our lives. Thank you, Jesus."

Psalm 27: 1
The Lord is my light and my salvation – whom shall I fear? The Lord is the stronghold of my life – of whom shall I be afraid?

'Just a Reminder-Each Day'

June 10

White

The definition of white has changed. Thanks to science, we know more about white and why ice crystals compacted together can look blue. Isaiah had a vision from God regarding Judah and Jerusalem which included this verse, Isaiah 1: 18 *'though your sins are like scarlet, they shall be as white as snow, though they are red as crimson, they shall be like wool'*. It seems to me that God had a very strong point to make and he used the most vivid contrasting descriptions that people of ancient times could understand.

When Jesus was transformed, the Bible says his clothes became dazzling white, whiter than anyone in the world could bleach them. Amusingly it is evident that once we add any colour to white paint, we can't bring it back to white. White is unique.

I am fortunate to have the use of cattle yards beside my stables. The big round rails look very impressive when painted white. Even better, they are the only thing you can see on a dark night so, at least, you know approximately where you are. White is impressive in so many ways like the bride walking down the aisle dressed in white or a huge fluffy white cloud floating across a dark blue sky.

There are times in our lives when we need to understand the power of God's forgiveness and how complete it is. Using 'white as snow' to describe how much we are forgiven still clearly shows us that nothing is left unforgiven. It is all washed clean.

"Lord God, some things we do wrong feel ugly and we regret them immensely. Thank you that you can take those burdens from us completely. Please help us to fully understand how complete your forgiveness is. Thank you, Jesus."

Ephesians 4: 32
Be kind and compassionate to one another, forgiving each other, just as in Christ God forgave you.

June 11

Overwhelmed

T here are times in our lives when we can feel quite overwhelmed by our circumstances. It may be an accumulation of events, personal, family, friends, community, national or even interna-tional concerns. When problems pile up and we feel it's all too much, it is in those times that we need to turn to like-minded friends, people who understand and support us in a way that works for us. Prayer support and encouraging words at the right time can give us the strength to continue.

Christianity is a network of positive values. Jesus demonstrated care for the individual and authority over evil. He introduced his Spirit as the Comforter, the One who leads us into the truth. The Holy Spirit helps us to get our concerns into perspective. He enables us to recognise those things that can be left behind. Moving from a stressful situation to a place of peace can be extremely difficult and take a long time, but God is the giver of real peace. Wait on him.

"Lord God, when worries of this world and in particular, my own world, consume me, please take charge of my life and bring your order and peace back into it. I trust you to do that which I can't do for myself. Thank you, Jesus."

Romans 8: 26
In the same way, the Holy Spirit helps us in our weakness. We do not know what we ought to pray for, but the Spirit himself intercedes for us with groans that words cannot express.

'Just a Reminder-Each Day'

Wind in My Face

I am sensitive to cold – a bit of a grump if I get too cold! I like to have a hat and coat handy to keep myself comfortable. I know it all sounds a bit wimpy but I've ended up feeling quite sick after a prolonged time in the cold. I am very grateful that the climate I grew up in and continue to live in is moderate. Another thing that makes me irritable is the unnecessary wind in my face. But I've ridden horses all my life and the moment you leave the sedate pace of walking you create wind – and that has never bothered me! Like when you are doing something you love, nothing else matters.

I was glad recently when our dog decided to race along the vast stretch of hard sand in pursuit of sea geese, which she never intended to catch. A gentle breeze hit me in the face as I watched her having fun. I was alone on the beach and the air pushing into my face felt like the presence of God! I soaked it up and asked him to fill me to overflowing with his goodness, even a week's worth, I suggested. He probably laughed, but he would have known what was on my mind. I was deeply concerned about a problem I had. I didn't have any answers and didn't know what I could do about it anyway.

]

"Lord God, you certainly surprise me sometimes. You meet us in ways that we don't expect. Thank you for all those times when you turn up with encouragement and your restoring Holy Spirit that drifts over us and through us, meeting our needs. Thank you, Jesus."

Psalm 16: 11
You have made known to me the path of life; you fill me with joy in your presence, with eternal pleasures at your right hand.

'Just a Reminder-Each Day'

Knock and Walk in

From the time I was first married, my in-laws had an open-door attitude in their home. I would knock once, announce my presence and walk in just like any other family member. My husband's married siblings have children, the number growing all the time, who also walk straight in! One reason why it works that way is the layout of the house. The first area is a closed-in veranda and the next is a wide passageway that leads in three different directions. At this point, your voice may be heard by those inside and, "It's only me" is a suitable announcement. Still, you are not expected to wait for someone to let you in. You just keep walking into the large, welcoming farm kitchen. Not only are family members always welcome but old friends and new friends too.

Jesus says he knocks! He doesn't just walk in! This Bible verse tells us so much about God's approach to us. He is a God who doesn't intrude into our lives. He waits to be invited in because it's the conversation and relationship that will develop, between those who open the door and Jesus who is knocking, that can be life changing. The verse also reads as if Jesus is continuously knocking. That's good news for all of us, considering how easy it is to be distracted and to put off opening our door to the most important guest we will ever have. Jesus is knocking.

"Lord God, thank you for graciously inviting us to know you and have a lifelong friendship. Please guard us against losing sight of what a privilege this is. Please help other people to hear you knocking. Thank you, Jesus."

Revelation 3: 20
Here I am! I stand at the door and knock. If anyone hears my voice and opens the door, I will come in and eat with him, and he with me.

'Just a Reminder-Each Day'

It starts at the Dinner Table

If it was not my mother reminding me to keep my elbows off the table or eat with my mouth shut, it was my grandmother telling me something else. Table manners were important in the home where I grew up. One thing that seemed to be missing in my childhood upbringing was the conversations about more profound things; like the purpose of life, where we came from, who oversees this world and even where we go when we die. I wonder if my father and mother had stayed together longer, would I have heard them talking about these issues? I notice now, in some homes, that these subjects do get addressed regularly. Parents talk about them openly. The very essence of Jesus' coming to earth is about his death and resurrection for our salvation. Hopefully, the deeper aspects of Christianity that didn't get discussed in my home, do get discussed in most Christian homes.

By exploring the meaning of life through faith in God and with instructions from the Bible, parents can set young people up with answers before they even ask questions. Children who hear these topics discussed are more likely to grow up feeling confident about life. I don't regret being taught good table manners, but it wasn't until I was an adult that God got my attention and revealed some important answers to life that surprised me.

"Lord God, I feel incredibly privileged to know your truth about life which gives me confidence for today and the future. Thank you for giving us an understanding of many of life's mysteries. Thank you, Jesus."

Luke 4: 18
Jesus read from the scroll – "The Spirit of the Lord is on me, because he has anointed me to preach good news to the poor. He has sent me to proclaim freedom for the prisoners and recovery of sight for the blind, to release the oppressed, to proclaim the year of the Lord's favour."

June 15
Patched up

My sewing machine gets neglected! I wouldn't say I like mending, but I'm also not in favour of throwing out clothes with holes in them if they can be patched. I'm not very tolerant of jeans with holes in the knees that fray and tear each time I bend down. Surprisingly, when I mend my jeans, the patches make them slightly heavier and quite a bit warmer for the winter. I like patched clothes!

My daily prayer list includes people from all parts of my life. Some I see often, others rarely. Some I pray for occasionally and others regularly. In all of us, there is some brokenness that needs fixing - some rips and tears that need patching up. It seemed like God was reminding me this morning to pray for patching up, not just for his protection over my list of people. When I view my own life, I am fully aware of how important each patch-up has been. I have gained confidence that a tear in my life ends up stronger if I get God to patch it up. Leaving hurts, disappointments, anger, frustration and brokenness unattended is more likely to worsen the situation, unless we go to God and get it patched up.

It is humiliating to own up to failure or any brokenness in our lives but there is total privacy in what we talk to God about, what we admit to and how he manages it.

Matthew 6:6 encourages us to go to our private place for prayer.

"Lord God, help us to take our needs to you without feeling a fool or a failure. Help us to receive the patch-up you always want for us. Thank you, Jesus."

1 Peter 5: 10,11
And the God of all grace, who called you to his eternal glory in Christ, after you have suffered a little while, will himself restore you and make you strong, firm, and steadfast. To him be the power for ever and ever. Amen.

June 16

Prayer – Try Again

Prayer can easily be seen as something weak people turn to—something mainly for women who just want to talk about their problems.

Once we were visiting a terminally ill person in a hospital and the subject of praying to God for help came up. The nurse who walked out with us said, "They all turn to God when they know they are dying." It seemed a harsh thing to say. The value of turning to God when we are in need says we credit God as being able to heal all manner of sickness, raise the dead, save souls for eternity and bring the earth to an end when he so wishes. Why wouldn't we pray?

Prayer gains power when prayers are answered. It is quite common for people to pray in a time of need, but a significant change happens when they realise their prayer has been answered. Even answers that don't turn out the way we want can still bring comfort and reassurance.

As the netball season rolled on, the team we were following were not looking like winning one game. Each time our goal shooter had a chance to throw a goal, we found ourselves willing the ball to just go through the hoop. We desperately wanted success. In one game, there was one rebound after another. Each one was caught by our goal shooter who, after four shots, managed to see the ball magically fall through the ring—the crowd ahh-ed with relief.

I am sure we have prayed one prayer after another, only to see it rebound and rebound again. A good aspect of asking God for something is that the rebounds are in his hands. The goal shooter could have given up and missed throwing a goal. We, too, need to keep praying because God always wants the best for us. Victory builds us up and restores our hope. Each prayer prayed gives an opportunity for an answered prayer and each answered prayer builds our faith for greater things.

"Lord God, please help us have the courage to ask and keep asking. Thank you, Jesus."

Luke 11: 10
For everyone who asks receives; he who seeks finds; and to him who knocks, the door will be opened.

'Just a Reminder-Each Day'

Footprints in the Sand

The local beach is quiet during the winter. The dog and I often have it to ourselves. I usually find myself checking for footprints in the sand as we make our way onto the beach, just in case another person has gone before us and let their dog loose to run on the wide expanse of sand. It was obvious that recent tides had been high in the evening, so I was amazed after careful examination to find a set of footprints in the wet sand that were mine from two days prior. 'Can this be?' I questioned myself as I checked and checked again the size and print of my boots. There was no doubt I was following in my own footprints! Immediately I thought of the writing called 'Footprints', by an unknown author, which has become quite famous. It tells of a dream where the person sees pictures of their life passing by each showing the footprints of Jesus walking with them, until a particularly difficult stage in the author's life where only one set of prints shows up in the sand. At this point, the author asks Jesus where he was in that difficult time. Jesus replies to the person, "During your time of trial and suffering, when you see only one set of footprints, it is then that I carried you."

In times when we want to stand firm or enter the battle to make a difference, it is then that we encounter another side of God. He battles on our behalf against the injustices of this world and equips us to fight for good and godly outcomes. The Old Testament tells stories of physical battles where the Israelites received divine help to have victory over their enemies. Those stories teach us how the Spirit of God works in people in their ordinary everyday battles. There are so many aspects to the nature of God that we can spend the rest of our lives discovering them. In today's culture of moral battles, we see that the living God (father and friend) is also the God of justice, truth and a fair go for everyone. He stands beside us, offers wisdom and gives us the courage to work for what is right. He is the game-changer!

"Lord God, thank you for arming us for battle. Thank you for giving us directions on when to fight and when to be passive. Thank you, Jesus."

Luke 10: 18,19
Jesus replied, "I saw Satan fall like lightning from heaven. I have given you authority to trample on snakes and scorpions and to overcome all the power of the enemy; nothing will harm you."

June 18

No Place to Call Home

Natural disasters happen all too often. In South Australia, we know all about fire, but floods are less frequent. When people suddenly lose a lot, sometimes everything they own, it affects their whole lives. It is often said that it is only material possessions, but the loss of businesses, farms, equipment, stock and homes changes people's lives immediately. We find so much of our daily identity through the house we live in, the tools we work with, the businesses we manage and the land we farm. A home is a place of shelter, a place to escape to and rest in and a welcoming environment for extended family and visitors. Our home is usually the place where we feel we belong.

There were several times in the Bible when people wanted to build a home or shelter for God, but he managed to convey to them that he did not need a home. In times of disaster, losing a home, pets, personal items and a place to work undermines people's confidence. We are not like God, who doesn't need a place to rest; we humans need a place to call home and the security of people and possessions around us.

Where is God in times of disaster? Where is his focus if he doesn't need a dwelling place like us? What gives him satisfaction? Is his life wrapped up in journeying with people, feeling their pain, sharing their highs and lows and picking up the pieces of those so badly hurt?

The world would like us to think that God doesn't care, but the response from people during and after a disaster suggests that both

God and people do care. There is an attitude common to Australians to 'help one another.' This mateship is based on Christian principles, and it is this mateship that will prevail.

"Lord God, please help us to identify with those who have lost their homes and possessions. Show us where we can help. Thank you, Jesus."

Lamentations 3: 31-33
For men are not cast off by the Lord forever. Though he brings grief, he will show compassion, so great is his unfailing love. For he does not willingly bring affliction or grief to the children of men.

'Just a Reminder-Each Day'

Pat the Cats!

I wandered down the veranda in the half-dark, my mind fixed on other things. On returning, I was surprised to notice that I had passed two cats, one sitting in a box ready for her evening snooze and the other on an old chair, also nestling down for a few hours of sleep. How is it that I didn't notice them the first time? They were so close that I could have reached out and patted them. It can be the same with God. He's close, but we don't notice him.

The apostle Paul in the book of Romans reassures his readers that nothing will ever separate them from the love of God. If we pass God by without noticing him, maybe we are the losers because he is there always!

If I walked past a friend in the street and ignored that friend because my mind was on other things, it would be rather rude, requiring an explanation and an apology. On the other hand, I probably pass God by quite regularly.

When I missed seeing the cats on the veranda, I missed the simple pleasure in life of patting them. If I miss the presence of God, I may well be missing a huge benefit to my life.

"Lord God, please help us to have our eyes open and to see where you are and what you are doing. We don't want to miss out on what you have planned for us and those we associate with. Thank you, Jesus."

Romans 8: 38,39
For I am convinced that neither death nor life, neither angels nor demons, neither the present nor the future, nor any powers, neither height nor depth, nor anything else in all creation, will be able to separate us from the love of God that is in Christ Jesus our Lord.

'Just a Reminder-Each Day'

June 20

A Voice to Share

The television show 'The Voice' exposes some hidden talent. One contestant admitted to not knowing why she had a good voice or what she was meant to do with it until she started singing in church. Christian judge Guy Sebastian responded, saying he understood because singing in church had helped him to see his voice was a gift to be shared. He admitted it was a humbling experience. The contestant said music was an amazing part of her life.

People, young and old, benefit when they realise they don't have gifts to gratify themselves alone. When our gifts are shared with others, and we acknowledge God as the giver of our gifts, it is like completing a jigsaw puzzle. It gives fulfilment.

Self-gratification is short-lived; it doesn't bring the true happiness we expect. A shared gift honours God and gives us satisfaction.

"Lord God, I thank you for all the gifts people share with others across society. Please help us to acknowledge that you are the giver of all good gifts. Please help us to use them wisely and confidently. Thank you, Jesus."

1 Peter 4:10
Each one should use whatever gift he has received to serve others, faithfully administering God's grace in its various forms-

June 21

Fight or Flight

I was surprised to see that my dog had chosen to stand by me rather than go on playing with my brother-in-law's dog. She had chosen the flight response rather than the fight. Sometimes she tells the other dog to leave her alone by snapping at him because he plays a bit rough for her liking. It can be quite unpleasant when dogs fight, especially when a dog dies or a human gets injured trying to split the fight up. There have been some worrying times on our farm when people have visited in their farm utilities with their dogs in the back; Our dogs would question their intentions.

The term fight or flight is often applied to men and women. Their response to conflict, solving problems and making decisions can often sort out which mechanism each person will employ. Men are most likely to choose to fight, while women may choose the flight response. But this is not a set reaction; some women will stay and fight while some men choose to move away.

How each person negotiates tricky situations in life can be so different. Still, a powerful way of resolving issues quietly and wisely can be experienced if both parties turn to God for his intervention.

During a church meeting where differences of opinion were being aired about a proposed change, I noticed that the main characters in the debate had narrowed down to five men and the women had taken a back seat. The fight mode had taken over. Fortunately, these men were open to God for their direction and the women stood by, still wanting a collective agreement. The outcome was agreeable. We can work together even if some choose to fight and others choose flight, but all choose to follow God.

"Lord God, we acknowledge the importance of those who choose to fight, those who have great courage and determination, while those who choose the flight action can take the heat out of the situation and allow peace to reign. Please help us to keep our actions and responses under your Lordship. Thank you, Jesus."

1 Corinthians 16: 13
Be on your guard, stand firm in the faith; be men of courage, be strong. Do everything in love.

Hope for a New House

Hope has a positive effect on people. Those in jail would surely hope to get out one day. Prisoners of war hang onto the hope that the war will end and they will return home safely. Children hope for presents at Christmas, and as adults, we all have something we hope for. Many people put their hope into winning the lottery. To hope in something can be useful or a waste of our thoughts and energy. I have probably wasted time drawing house plans in the hope of one day building a new house. I have loved thinking about the best possible plan and going over it again and again, trying to make it better. Sometimes I wonder what I would place my hopes on if we did build our house, but then I am reminded of the things God has already surprised me with. I never thought I would spend hours at my computer printing up these 'Reminders'.

The idea of creating a daily devotion with a Bible reading barely ever entered my head until a friend prayed for us. I had admitted to him that I felt I was at a crossroads and needed something of value to do. It was shortly after PK had prayed for my husband and me (that evening when I was preparing tea) that I thought God said, "I am going to give you 365 daily devotions. Just quickly write them down when I give them to you, use anything to record them, don't worry about typing them on the computer, just on a scrap of paper, serviette, whatever you can find at the time." Later that evening, while stirring the tea, I received a thought, wrote it down and then received another. A similar pattern happened until one year and one month later I found myself writing the 365th article of **'Just a Reminder – Each Day'.**

This project has given me considerable satisfaction and restored my hope of being a useful Christian.

"Lord God, you know we need hope. All people need some form of hope. Thank you for the hope that comes directly from you to us. Please restore hope where it is lacking in our family, church, community, nation, and world. Thank you, Jesus."

Proverbs 13: 12
Hope deferred makes the heart sick, but a longing fulfilled is a tree of life.

June 23

Not Aware

During a radio interview with an author, the interviewer added his own experience. "I heard an author once say that the words he wrote for his character to say turned out to be good advice for his own life; have you ever written something and then realised it was surprisingly good for you personally?" Silence! The interviewer continued, "Perhaps you might wonder where some lines come from when you are writing." A shorter silence this time, then the reply, "No, I don't think I have ever had that experience." It was an almost embarrassing moment for the interviewer. He certainly didn't get the response he was after. The author did not give any credit to God, or any other outside influence that may have put the ideas into her mind.

Christians often attribute thoughts or ideas that seem to come from nowhere as coming from the Holy Spirit. Why wouldn't God implant ideas into our lives without us asking for them? God, who is always attentive to us, would surely take opportunities to expand our experience. Maybe, sometimes, we try too hard to hear God, to get his direction for our lives instead of just expecting the unexpected. The Holy Spirit is called the Comforter, Counsellor and the One who leads us into the truth. Jesus was a friend who comforted and counselled his followers, so I am encouraged that we can expect the same relationship with his Spirit.

"Lord God, what a privilege to have your ideas come into our thinking. What comfort and encouragement to have your Spirit to relate to and inspire us. Thank you, Jesus."

John 14: 26
(Jesus said) But the counsellor, the Holy Spirit, whom the Father will send in my name, will teach you all things and remind you of everything I have said to you.

'Just a Reminder-Each Day'

June 24

Mid-night Max

So many people living in and around our town had sighted the stray dog. His owner, from a town 100 kilometres away, had stopped for fuel at a service centre on the outskirts of the town. Max was released from his cage but took off and would not respond to being called back. The owner saw his dog running down the highway with motorists tooting at him. Over several weeks many attempts, by the owner and the council, had failed to catch the dog.

Apparently, Max had been moving around the district very discreetly for nearly three months, finding food where he could, before we had our first encounter with him. Max was upset! The battle to survive in a strange place had caused him to fear being caught.

One day we discovered the bag of dry dog food in our car shed had been dragged around. On a very cold night, from our front window, we saw a wet, black dog curled up tight on our couch on the veranda. Moved with compassion, like many other animal lovers around the town, we tried to befriend Max. But as soon as we opened the door he fled. We persevered, leaving dry food available and eventually raw meat. He got used to our routine and started arriving well before midnight. It saddened us as we observed him wake at dawn and head off- to where we didn't know. When my slippers went missing and were found in the park across from our house, we realised this stray dog, although fully grown, was still a pup. After a week or two, he moved to our car shed and tried to share the bed with our dog, so I created two beds. From there he started sleeping in a bit. Another week passed and I was able to offer him some meat for breakfast before he ran away. It proved to be an emotional strain wondering when and if the dog would ever completely trust us. The morning Max greeted us with his tail wagging and allowed us to pat him was the greatest reward. That first pat revealed how much this dog was starved of love and security. We had the pleasure of another week with Max, our stray dog, but we knew we had to return him to his home.

"Lord God, thank you for the privilege of being able to help out when someone or something is in need. Thank you, Jesus."

Psalm 143: 8
Let the morning bring me word of your unfailing love, for I have put my trust in you.

'Just a Reminder-Each Day'

June 25
Advance Australia Fair

With God or without God? It is a free choice. We sing our anthem with confidence that we are advancing just the way we want to; other people may think differently. If there were no God, our advancing would be man driven. But the truth is, as I see it, God, the Living God, creator of all that exists, cares intimately for our nation and us and he is with us.

There is an attitude that we can live without acknowledging God, do it all ourselves and who cares – we are advancing on our own and we are doing fine. Or are we?

God is not a dictator, he gives us free will, so it may seem we can advance without him if we want. He is completely fair. He sends rain on the just and unjust, those who acknowledge him and those who do not.

Our nation may be advancing unaware of any help from God. We believe in his involvement by faith, not necessarily by sight, and as a result, God will be praised by some people and not by others.

We could sing our anthem to acknowledge God by changing a few words.

'In step with God, then let us sing.'

Advance Australia fair. (You may have better ideas)

For those of us who have found faith in Jesus, the need to acknowledge God and honour him is a prerequisite to our advancing anywhere.

It takes courage to stand up for what we believe and admit we don't want to advance anywhere unless Jesus leads us, personally and as a nation.

"Lord God, you are the head of our nation, the God of all gods, and we choose to honour and respect you. Thank you, Jesus."

Psalm 22: 27,28
All the ends of the earth will remember and turn to the Lord, and all the families of the nations will bow down before him, for dominion belongs to the Lord and he rules over the nations.

My Sheep Know My Voice

How impressive that the Bible is the living word of God! My favourite verses are John 10: 3, 14 & 15; the fact that God knows me personally among the millions on earth is rather astounding. From the first time, those Bible verses hit home with me and gave me the warm fuzzy feeling of being His, to now, those verses are still alive and meaningful. It convinces me of God's desire for an intimate relationship with each person. I get it. It does me good.

A mob of sheep paints a uniform picture. It appears as a ripple of pale greyish-white wool or brownish, depending on what area you are in. If there is a pet sheep in the mob, it will step away from the mob and make itself known to its human family. It then becomes an individual. We may think we can pick out our pet sheep from the mob, but it's not until they pick us out that we can be sure we have the right one.

God proves his interest in us as individuals when he picks us out and calls us by name. We need to take Bible verses like this one seriously because this world can undermine our confidence in our rightful place with God. This scripture is for our sake so we can know, without a doubt, that God knows us and cares for us.

A pet sheep's confidence in its owners is a good example of how we can trust God. We had one pet sheep who knew how to avoid all the harassment from the sheepdogs and us. He would push through the mob and get drafted first then all the others would follow him! Very helpful sheep! Another pet wether we had, chose to walk with us, while we were trying to herd the others through the drafting gate. Consequently, all the sheep thought they could stay back with us, too. We soon realised that one of us needed to take the pet sheep through the draft and get it out of the way. That sheep was too clingy!

"Lord God, please help us to hear your voice and trust you even when something is harassing us from behind. Help us to go straight to you for comfort and protection because you know us. Thank you, Jesus."

John 10: 3, 14 & 15
The watchman opens the gate for him, and the sheep listen to his voice. He calls his own sheep by name and leads them out. I am the good shepherd; I know my sheep and my sheep know me - just as the Father knows me and I know the Father - and I lay down my life for the sheep.

June 27

I don't Need It (said the Lord)

The dog and I had the beach to ourselves. A sense of peace and gratitude swept over me as I walked onto the damp sand. The tide was out, allowing the dog space to run almost out of sight. I clicked my camera a few times, trying to capture the beauty of the pale blue water pools and perfectly patterned sand. I briefly told the Lord I was ready to hear him if he had things to tell me. I waited and heard nothing. I wandered and listened and still heard nothing. So, I reminded him, in the peace and tranquillity of the beach, that it was an ideal time to show me something.

I wandered a little further, watched the dog and heard nothing from God. I was a bit surprised because I thought he would take the opportunity to speak when he had my full attention.

I gave up listening and just wrote in the sand, 'Great is the Lord', then I drew a happy face. Not very inspiring, I know. Then it seemed to me that God said, "I don't need it, this peace and quiet. I can talk to you and get your attention in any circumstances."

Well, I didn't see that coming! But I knew I was getting reminded of who was calling the shots. My God can't be manipulated, won over or told what to do. He is above all our earthly ways and restrictions.

"Lord God, just when we think we know you, we realise we hardly know you at all. Please continue to teach us everything we need to understand about you. Thank you, Jesus."

Romans 11: 33-36 (the writer has taken quotes from Isaiah and Job)
Oh, the depth of the riches of the wisdom and knowledge of God!
How unsearchable his judgements, and his paths beyond tracing out!
"Who has known the mind of the Lord? Or who has been his counsellor?"
"Who has ever given to God, that God should repay him?"
For from him and through him and to him are all things.
To him be the glory for ever! Amen.

'Just a Reminder-Each Day'

June 28

Muddy Roads

Young drivers can have many outcomes in the early days of driving on public roads. Most country children have driven on someone's farm before they are at the age of getting a licence. Those raised on farms are usually driving confidently at 12-14 years old, some earlier. Some young drivers with no experience are far too confident. Some think they know how but still make mistakes, while others are tentative, anxious and too scared to be reliable.

My first bad experience was in wet conditions on a muddy dirt road. I had lost control of the car. Landing on the bank was uneventful as I had been going very slowly. After I married, negotiating muddy farm tracks was a safer way of gaining experience. My husband was more than happy to instruct me on the way to keep some forward movement without getting stuck. I learnt through instruction, and plenty of practice with various vehicles, that keeping one wheel on some solid ground while keeping up enough pace to avoid getting bogged was good. Going too fast and spinning into the fence was not the way to go. Every wet winter has had its challenges. I did notice, however, that the men and boys behind the wheel found the challenge a lot more fun than I did.

Negotiating the rough patches in life is a bit like getting through muddy roads. With the right instructions, we can keep the vehicle going straight and forward, but without it, we may just end up in the fence. That is why I appreciate being able to go to Jesus for help. I am glad

I have improved at driving in muddy situations, but I would not have if my husband had just taken over and done that section of driving for me. In the same way, God teaches us how to negotiate life. He doesn't do it for us, but he is always there to show us how. He doesn't promise we won't get bogged or need someone to pull us out. The experience and instruction along the way are all part of our relationship with God.

"Lord God, please help us enjoy the journey with you, learn how to negotiate the muddy patches and appreciate your guidance. Thank you, Jesus."

Psalm 40:2
He lifted me out of the slimy pit, out of the mud and mire; he set my feet on a rock and gave me a firm place to stand.

June 29
Feel Good Faith

The television remote control is a treasured possession if we are about to choose which movie we want to watch. It happens between couples, in families and among groups of friends. The men are focused on something with a challenge, a battle requiring courage, but the women want a feel-good, romantic, happy ending movie. It can lead to some friendly rivalry as the choice is made.

The gospel of Jesus Christ is not only a feel-good faith but also a battle between good and evil. Jesus has won the victory for us. Standing up for something we believe in can put us under attack. Feeling good about our faith in God and doing battle for his kingdom

should coexist. God is the God of all people. It is essential that we feel good in our relationship with God and understand the grace he extends to us. It is through his Fatherly love that his eternal plan (happy ending) is on offer. It is also essential that we recognise the battlefield, the ongoing fight against evil that Jesus equips us for and the victory Jesus has won for all who believe. The remote is in our hands: Choose God.

"Lord God, thank you for the encouragement to feel good about our faith and also stand against injustices in your name. Please empower others who need to know they can have victory over their enemy. Thank you, Jesus."

1 John 5: 4
For everyone born of God, overcomes the world. This is the victory that has overcome the world, even our faith.

June 30

House Rules

During the winter of one year, a family with small children came to stay at our farm. We enjoyed showing them around the property but when we were indoors it was very cold unless certain doors were kept shut. Our thick limestone walls with high ceilings and doors that let cold air in meant that we had to follow some rules to keep the house warm. With only one small wood fire that worked quite inefficiently, it was always hard to keep the warmth where we needed it.

Our visitors were seated in the kitchen enjoying morning tea with us. I was quite surprised and impressed when their children came running from the bedroom area to the kitchen and their mother quickly told them to shut the door behind them. 'Wow, how considerate!' I thought to myself, but then I remembered that their home was very similar to ours and they were used to the same house rules we upheld. We enjoyed their company and hoped we had been able to give them some valuable respite.

In the following Bible reading, Jesus knew that Zacchaeus would welcome him into his house. It would be a profitable visit. Zacchaeus was ready to know Jesus and make his life right with God.

"Lord God, show us the people we should welcome into our homes, those who will benefit from spending time with us and those who are our like-minded support people. Thank you, Jesus."

Luke 19: 1-6

Jesus entered Jericho and was passing through. A man was there by the name of Zacchaeus; he was a chief tax collector and was wealthy. He wanted to see who Jesus was, but being a short man, he could not, because of the crowd. So he ran ahead and climbed a sycamore-fig tree to see him, since Jesus was coming that way. When Jesus reached the spot, he looked up and said to him, "Zacchaeus, come down immediately. I must stay at your house today." So he came down at once and welcomed him gladly.

'Just a Reminder-Each Day'